What People Are Sayin

If It's Tuesday

I was enchanted by the novel. I thought it had magic, freedom, poignancy, and not least, brilliant and evocative backdrops. It's unusual and fluent, and I was captivated.
Elizabeth Buchan, author of *Bonjour, Sophie*

Nooteboom-inflected European mystery tour? Your guide, the beguiling Tony Peake? Where do I sign?
Nicholas Royle, author of *Shadow Lines*

If It's Tuesday

A Novel

If It's Tuesday

A Novel

Tony Peake

ROUNDFIRE
BOOKS

London, UK
Washington, DC, USA

CollectiveInk

First published by Roundfire Books, 2025
Roundfire Books is an imprint of Collective Ink Ltd.,
Unit 11, Shepperton House, 89 Shepperton Road, London, N1 3DF
office@collectiveinkbooks.com
www.collectiveinkbooks.com
www.roundfire-books.com

For distributor details and how to order please visit the 'Ordering' section on our website.

Text copyright: Tony Peake 2024

ISBN: 978 1 80341 904 6
978 1 80341 913 8 (ebook)
Library of Congress Control Number: 2024942164

A CIP catalogue record for this book is available from the British Library.

Design: Lapiz Digital Services

UK: Printed and bound by CPI Group (UK) Ltd, Croydon, CR0 4YY
Printed in North America by CPI GPS partners

We operate a distinctive and ethical publishing philosophy in
all areas of our business, from our global network of authors to
production and worldwide distribution.

The use of travelling is to regulate imagination by reality, and instead of thinking how things may be, to see them as they are.
— **Samuel Johnson,** in a letter to Hester Thrale

All travel is the pursuit of magic.
— **Duncan Fallowell,** *To Noto*

The world is full of magic things, patiently waiting for our senses to grow sharper.
— commonly attributed to **W.B. Yeats**

Contents

Day 1

It being a Tuesday, as Cody stood by the curtains that wholly covered one wall of his hotel room, hand fumbling in the folds at their edge for a drawstring, he was fleetingly reminded of a certain film before all the more important stuff came crowding in. Like: where exactly were they? He'd need to establish that in order to suggest an itinerary. And what, over all, should he expect of the trip ahead? How much would be more or less as anticipated? How much would catch him (and the others) unawares? What highs, what lows? Would it be a week to welcome? Or one to file away afterwards in the drawer marked 'could do better'?

He'd woken early and, on sitting up, had immediately scanned the room he found himself in – as usual, he'd no memory of going to sleep there; waking was what had brought his surroundings into focus – for some give-away. All he saw, though, was a featureless built-in cupboard; a flat-screen television; a generic desk unit containing a mini-bar; a kettle and the minimal means of making tea or coffee; those curtains. He could have been almost anywhere. So, shucking off the covers, he leapt up, stretched and went at once to find a drawstring that, when yanked, would reveal all.

The resulting view, of a tree-lined canal, quite wide, the water iridescent with morning light, was picturesque in the extreme. Small boats, some shrouded in tarpaulin, some with cabins, others little better than skiffs, were moored at regular intervals along both banks. There were lines too of parked cars under the trees, but no traffic on the cobbled streets that ran on either side of the canal. To his right, an arched bridge spanned the rippling water, stone built, with a collection of largely black bicycles leaning against or chained to its iron railings.

Not Belgium, then. But close.

In the bathroom, Cody considered another view. The one in the mirror above the basin. Less than picturesque, perhaps, although he supposed it wasn't too bad for a man past the first flush of youth. Hair in blond abundance, with the lines around his eyes and mouth suggesting character over age. The fact that he'd lived a little; was not without experience.

He began shaving. *Nu dan!* What should it be today? The Anne Frank House was normally on someone's list. The Rijksmuseum too. And Van Gogh of course. The flower market? Or would this week's group surprise him? As yet, he'd no way of knowing. All he'd been given were their names and the barest of biographical details. More would come later.

So! There was a Simon, in his early twenties and apparently the nephew of (or anyway related to; on this detail Cedric had been unaccountably vague) the only female present, name of Margaret. Plus Geoffrey, a teacher on sabbatical. His tightest group in ages. Although this didn't for one moment mean he wouldn't have his work cut out. Often the smallest groups were the most demanding, everyone imagining you had time just for them, and them alone.

Drying his face on one of those towels whose ebullient fluffiness indicated a hotel provenance – most domestic towelling being nothing like as luxuriant in his experience – Cody looked deep into the green of his own eyes. Leprechaun's eyes, someone had once remarked. Not altogether approvingly, either.

***

In an identical room on the floor below, Simon was trapped in the dream he'd been experiencing on and off for some time now. In it, he was wandering, lost, through an unknown city. Empty but for him and his echoing footsteps. And today, another sound as well: lapping water, except he couldn't for the life of him see from where it was emanating.

Hesitantly, he advanced into a square, buildings on every side, although their architectural details remained vague. He was aware only of tallness and bulk; not what the buildings truly looked like.

Then he saw it. A distant flash of navy blue, which he knew to be a coat of some sort, worn by the only person who could ever lead him out of this intimidating emptiness towards other people and signs of life, all the elements you might expect to find in a city, but never did in Simon's dream.

He wondered how things would pan out on this occasion? For sometimes, after running towards the flash of blue, breath coming in hopeful yet panicked bursts, he was allowed virtually to touch the coat. While at others, it would vanish even as he glimpsed it.

Today, he was within inches, had merely to stretch out his hand and he'd have been able to arrest the fleeing figure, spin them round to see who his potential saviour actually was. Then he heard a knocking and meddlesome Aunt Margaret was murmuring through the door: 'Simon, dear, I hope this is you? I did particularly ask for us to be put next to each other. Just popping out for a bit. See you at breakfast. All right?'

Surfacing, Simon felt a flash of annoyance. Bloody Auntie M with her absolute knack for intruding when you least wanted her to. When you maybe stood a chance at last of reaching out and touching the coat and... whereas all he currently saw, as he lay there motionless, was the fleshy darkness of his inner eyelids, drawn like a red curtain across any kind of outcome.

Then he began scolding himself for being so churlish. He'd much, almost too much, to thank his aunt for. Even if it did come at a price. Like asking him to accompany her on a week-long mystery tour of Europe. New horizons, she'd said, never to be sniffed at and she did sometimes sense – was she wrong? – that he was marking time. Not only at the garden centre, but elsewhere too.

Yes? Am I guessing right, Simon, dear?

Opening his eyes, he decided to establish how far they had in fact travelled overnight, since at a glance he could obviously tell they were no longer at home. So he drew back the curtains of his unfamiliar hotel room to reveal the canal, the boats, the bicycles on the bridge, plus gabled buildings whose architectural nuances – unlike those in his dream – were immediately evident. And as he absorbed the pleasing scene, he couldn't help but agree with his generous yet infuriating aunt that although they'd patently not come far, just the shortest of hops from Suffolk, it was nonetheless true about new horizons. A small boat was nosing into the centre of the canal, causing the water to sparkle, and someone in a yellow blouse was cycling gaily across the bridge. Sights he would never in a million years have seen back home. He felt a quickening.

***

Margaret was wanting a church: the Catholic kind, which she thought might be harder to find in a protestant city than in Rome, say, the only European capital she knew at all well. So, on her way through the lobby, she'd asked at reception and they'd obligingly shown her on a map exactly where she needed to head. Just one canal away. That's all.

This was a favourite time of day for Margaret. Everything to hope for still and if the day itself didn't ultimately deliver, for the moment at least you weren't to know. A rising sun, a blue sky and who cared if the air stayed chilly – the night hadn't quite relinquished its hold – because she'd had the foresight, thank goodness, to wear a cardigan.

There was a bridge to the right of the hotel, which she took as instructed and so on along a narrow street paved in red brick, with tall, narrow houses to either side, some containing shops. She passed a bakery, its doors open and that alluring smell of freshly baked bread; a shuttered hardware store; a Thai takeaway. Then the next canal, where she was supposed to turn left; and already she could see a steep grey roof towering above the other buildings in the middle distance. But so agreeable was it to be walking in the early morning through an unknown and unexpected city that she decided to turn right and go instead to another bridge before zeroing in on her destination.

Here was where she encountered the bicycle. A bell rang and she found herself in the path of a contraption that looked more like a wheelbarrow. A woman in a yellow blouse, ramrod straight, was riding it, sat behind a low wooden receptacle fixed between the wheels, in which were heaped three small children in brightly coloured tops. Like their mother – assuming the woman to be their mother; but why wouldn't she be? – they were all blond and they all waved at her as she stepped aside. There was a snatch of giggling and the woman smiled gratefully too. Though what really captured Margaret's attention was that one of the children looked so like Simon at a similar age. The same untidiness of hair. The same eager eyes and half open mouth. Well, as photographed anyway.

The church, when eventually she reached it, was a soaring affair, ornately decorated and with a trio of stained glass windows behind the altar that rose all the way to the vaulted ceiling. Personally, she would have preferred somewhere smaller; somewhere simpler; she mistrusted ecclesiastical grandstanding. She'd also been hoping for a mass, although according to the board outside, for that she'd have had to wait until 12.30. Now she must make do with joining a small handful of other worshippers, all female, none particularly young-looking, each knelt in a separate pew in silent, head-bowed prayer. Too early still for tourists.

The stained glass was ablaze with light and it was on this trinity of tall windows that Margaret concentrated while making the sign of the cross. As always, she prayed first for Simon; specifically, that this trip they were making might trigger an unlocking. She could tell that something was troubling him, even though he hadn't ever confided in her. Maybe on the road he could be encouraged to open up? Then, one by one, she remembered all the other people she routinely included in her prayers. Her dead sister and brother-in-law. The children from Buenos Aires, name by name where she could. Even Gustavo. Coming to herself only as an afterthought and without once questioning how the trip could have started without preamble. Some things you just had to take on faith.

***

Having prepared himself a not very enticing cup of coffee from the paltry ingredients to hand, Geoffrey was in his pyjamas at the desk unit below the television screen, CNN dishing out news. But without any sound because Geoffrey didn't want distracting while writing up his journal. An early morning task he habitually set himself these days, now that he didn't have to rush off and teach.

Being on sabbatical did not, however, seem to make much difference and he stared in mounting frustration at the virgin page. *Tuesday*, it said. But that was all. And this despite a most promising change of scene – he'd drawn the curtains already – plus the prospect of a whole week of new and possibly quite exotic adventures. Arrived at furthermore in a highly unusual manner, worth pondering in and of itself. What was the matter with him? Why couldn't he express himself? Was it really too much to ask? A daily quota of words?

He consulted yesterday's entry, which ended hopefully: *So much time, what a gift! Time to think, expand, explore.*

Then he heard Isobel say, in a sneering tone: 'Or fritter it all away, more like. Going on past experience.'

He looked sharply upwards, fully expecting to see her on the TV. For that's how it had sounded. As if she were somehow in the room with him. But no, the woman on his screen looked nothing like his ex-wife. She'd blonde hair, for a start, a far softer face and anyway, the sound was turned down. Isobel was addressing him from inside his own head.

'Sometimes you do amuse me, Geoffrey. Really you do.'

He took his coffee to the window, where, as he waited fretfully for his thoughts to settle, he noticed an attractive-looking middle-aged woman in a beige cardigan and a summery skirt cross a nearby bridge to vanish up the street that adjoined it. Two years already! Two whole years since Isobel had run off with Howard. And still she spoke to him internally, enumerating his deficiencies with disquieting insight and relish.

Wistfully, he thought back to the early days, to a basement flat off Stoke Newington High Street with so much mould on the bathroom ceiling that they'd wittily thought of it as a design feature. Back then, he'd had her warm support as he wrestled with the important novel he was nurturing about a newly married couple living in a basement flat off Stoke Newington High Street. Write what you know. So he had. And where had it got him? Or was the real mistake to have rented the spare room to a graphic designer called Howard?

Turning in despair from the window, Geoffrey went back to his journal and looked again at the single word on the page before him. *Tuesday*. And next? Where next? What would it take to make the words flow? Maybe if he paid fuller attention to exactly how he'd been whisked to Amsterdam, maybe that would do the trick? It was a key requirement, after all, for any writer: being properly observant.

***

Breakfast was a buffet. A large table in the centre of a large room displayed a tempting arrangement of food, the only drawback being that not all of the guests went round it in the same direction. There was always someone who zipped in front of you; or else they wanted you to step aside as they moved from cereal to fruit while you progressed from fruit to cereal. But then, thought Geoffrey, as he managed to help himself to some muesli at last, orderly queuing was the province of the tribe who lived in splendid isolation across the water and if any Europeans had ever felt the need to show solidarity with this most Anglo-Saxon of traits, presumably – post-Brexit – that need had now been nullified.

He checked the contents of his tray. Orange juice, a banana, the muesli and a small pot of vanilla yoghurt. Coffee he could always get later. Or did they just bring that to your table? Which led him to wonder where best to sit. Was there a designated spot perhaps? So much remained uncertain about this trip. It hurt his head to even think about it.

A man with an impressive mane of blond hair, dressed all in white – white T-shirt, white jeans, white sneakers – was by a table in the furthest corner of the room, waving with intent.

'Morning!' he beamed as Geoffrey approached. 'Name's Cody. Your guide for the week ahead. Nice to meet you. Geoffrey, yes?'

Geoffrey nodded.

'The others will be with us shortly, I'm sure.'

'Others? How many?'

'Oh, just two this time. A guy called Simon and...' Here Cody's eyes – a startling green, Geoffrey noticed – flicked sideways as he gave another of his commanding waves. 'There he is now, I think.'

Coming towards them was a trim figure, neatly attired in chinos and a button-down shirt, also carrying a tray, although unlike Geoffrey, this member of the group had gone for the continental option: rolls, ham, cheese. And to drink, some sort of

8

smoothie, thick enough to support upright the straw emerging like a pole from its peachy depths.

'You must be Simon,' said their guide. 'This is Geoffrey. I'm Cody. We're just missing your...'

'Aunt, yes,' said the young man, acknowledging Geoffrey with a shy but appealing smile as he took the seat opposite. 'She's gone out. Looking for a church most probably, knowing Auntie M. Don't worry, though. She won't be long. Being late is her absolute worst. Major no-no.'

He cut into a roll, then carefully unwrapped one of the half a dozen or so miniature parcels of butter he had on his tray. His hair was cut very short – a number one or two – and Geoffrey could see every ridged detail of his skull, plus two pinkish ears in their entirety.

Sensing that he was under scrutiny, Simon looked up from his plate. His eyes – large, brown, mournful – met Geoffrey's unblinkingly.

'Unlike me at your age,' said Geoffrey with a sudden, surprised laugh, 'you're clearly someone who thinks ahead.'

'Sorry?'

Geoffrey gestured at Simon's tray. 'The butters.'

Simon now began his own assessment of the older man. The T-shirt that didn't quite hide where Geoffrey's stomach was starting to spread; a few patches of greying stubble missed by his razor; a pair of fashionably heavy-rimmed glasses that tried – too hard perhaps? – to deflect attention from these signs of ageing. And hanging from his chair, a leather shoulder bag, quite battered-looking.

'When I was in my twenties,' continued Geoffrey, sounding a rueful note, 'if I thought ahead, it was the next significant pleasure I invariably had in mind. The next excitement. Precautions, safeguards, were seldom taken.'

'Well, you can always help yourself to some of mine if you're short,' volunteered Simon. 'I guess I have been a bit greedy.'

'Is that maybe her?'

The question came from Cody, who was pointing to where the woman Geoffrey had seen on the bridge earlier was standing by the buffet with a tray of her own, anxiously scanning the breakfast room.

'Yes,' confirmed Simon, looking up from his many butters. 'That's Auntie M.'

Cody rose and, as the woman, who'd meanwhile seen them, started in their direction, so began yet another scrutiny, conducted by three pairs of eyes this time. Simon looked for what mood his aunt might be in. Cody saw not only the woman's anxiety, but beyond that to what he guessed might be a more permanent condition of sadness and regret. While Geoffrey, as he took in the floral skirt and blouse and beige cardigan, wondered why such an attractive woman – good cheekbones, a generous mouth, lovely hair, he even liked the grey – should choose to dress so mutedly.

'Right!' pronounced Cody, once Margaret had joined them and the necessary introductions had been effected and everyone was comfortably seated. 'So here we all are then. Time to begin!'

***

A waitress took their orders for coffee and tea, after which Cody started his customary spiel by emphasising that the success of the tour would depend mostly on them. He said he'd always be there, of course, to facilitate matters and he hoped they'd always feel free to turn to him when needed. But for the rest, *they* were in the driving seat. *They* were the nucleus.

'These mystery tours we run,' he explained, without once mentioning how long he'd been a guide, or who he worked for, 'they're all about you. Your needs. Your hopes. Your aspirations. I'm just the enabler. And although the uncertainty isn't easy to cope with, I do appreciate that, especially at first, you'll find that it's actually a vital part of how we do things. None of you know what you might discover. And quite frankly, neither do I in many cases. That's rather the point. We're on a journey together and if you give yourselves over to the journey, uncertainties included, you'll be surprised at what you might learn. How you might emerge on the other side.'

'Younger would be good,' quipped Geoffrey, grinning wolfishly at Margaret.

'Anything's possible,' smiled Cody. 'Within reason. It's like reading a book. You open it without any idea of where it might carry you, but as long as you let the story take hold – and it's persuasive enough, of course – then the sky's the limit.'

'So what I'd like to know,' said Simon, settling for the most straightforward of questions in the face of all the other, more intricate and puzzling things he might have asked, 'is why Amsterdam? To kick off with, I mean. Some special reason? Or are we here just by chance?'

The waitress arrived with their order. She was very young and it seemed as though this could be her first job, even the first day of her first job, because serving appeared to fluster her unduly and, in transferring their cafetiere from her tray to the centre of the table, she almost succeeded in knocking it over. Geoffrey leaped up, although this just complicated matters in that his elbow then caught the edge of the waitress's tray and if Simon's own reactions had been any slower, Margaret's tea might have been delivered directly into her lap.

'*Iartă-mă!*' exclaimed the unnerved waitress, stepping backwards as Simon shot out a hand, arrested the cup mid-slide and handed it to his aunt himself.

'No harm done,' said Simon. 'Hey, Auntie M?'

But the waitress wasn't mollified. 'I so sorry,' she mumbled. 'Very, how you say…?'

'And I'm sorry,' said Simon promptly, 'about my lack of Dutch. We English…'

'Although I think you'll find,' said Cody quietly, 'that it's Romanian.'

'Romanian?'

'Ah-ha!' cried Geoffrey, who'd sat down again. 'In which case: some *zahăr* please! If you wouldn't mind.' He turned confidingly to Margaret as the waitress hastened off to fulfil his request. 'I've a wickedly sweet tooth, so what I did once was teach myself the word for sugar in all the European languages. Romanian included.'

'How very enterprising,' said Margaret.

'Well, when it comes to my own wants,' replied Geoffrey with another lupine grin, 'my own desires...' He gave an eloquent shrug.

'Talking of wants and desires,' said Cody, 'what's on everyone's list for Amsterdam? Would it help to run through some options perhaps?' There was no longer any need, he hoped, to return to Simon's essentially unanswerable question as to why they were starting here. The waitress's clumsiness had conveniently wiped that awkward little slate clean. 'The museums are all open,' he went on, 'it's usually only on a Monday that they close on the continent. So we're secure on that front at least. Or do we prefer outdoors? The weather should stay fine. Right! Who'd like to start?'

*****

In the end, they decided on the Anne Frank house for the morning – everyone wanted that – and, in the afternoon, probably an art museum. Simon and Geoffrey both favoured van Gogh, but Margaret was keener on the Rijksmuseum. In particular, a work by Rembrandt that she'd read about. *The Jewish Bride.* 'As it's commonly called.'

'Well, when it comes to Rembrandt,' said Geoffrey, 'all I'd bloody recognise is *The Night Watch*. Sort of.'

'So my awesome aunt here,' said Simon with an admiring smile, 'has always been really up on her art. Haven't you, Auntie M?'

'But I'd hate to spoil things for everyone else,' said Margaret quickly. 'If van Gogh gets the majority vote, that's quite all right by me. Or the flower market even. I wouldn't mind the flower market. And I know that you, Simon, would like that too. Wouldn't you, dear?'

'No, no,' said Geoffrey. 'Now you've intrigued me. The Rijksmuseum it is. Okay, Simon? And pass the *zahăr*, will you?' He'd emptied the dregs from the cafetiere into his cup. 'Sorry, did anyone else want seconds? I can always ask our pretty young waitress.'

'No need,' said Margaret tightly. 'I've had my fill.'

'Me too,' said Simon, passing Geoffrey the sugar.

'I'm also wondering,' put in Cody, 'what thoughts you might have, each of you, about where you'd like to go next? After Amsterdam. Any special places? Things to do. Things to see. Like Margaret with her Rembrandt. Or avoid doing. Avoid seeing.'

'You mean the choice is wholly up to us?' The woman in question sounded not just mystified, but amazed even. Disbelieving too.

Cody fixed her with a penetrating stare. 'Who did I say was in the driving seat?'

There was a pause.

'Ah, yes,' she said finally, as if hypnotised. 'Of course. The nucleus. You did mention that.'

'I'm sorry,' said Cody, continuing to stare. 'The first day is always hard. But if you can all three just go with the flow...' His stare widened, taking in each of them in turn.

There was another pause, broken eventually by Geoffrey.

'So for me,' he said, 'it would have to be Paris.'

'Can you tell us why?'

Geoffrey took a considered sip of his coffee. How to start? As he'd done sometimes in the staff common room, if the question ever arose? With the usual, jokey deflections? Can-Can, the Moulin Rouge, ooh-la-la. Or was now the moment to admit – taking his lead from Margaret, in a way, apropos the Rijksmuseum – that he wouldn't automatically head for the Mona Lisa when visiting the Louvre? How to be honest? That was the crux of it. How honest to be.

'If you're even remotely capable,' sniped Isobel internally. 'In that regard.'

'So!' he began. 'Okay!' Already the words felt heavy in his mouth, like stones. 'Ever since I can remember, from when I was a youngster, what I've wanted more than anything – and I mean anything; it's with me all the time – is to be a writer.' There! He'd said it. And to a tableful of strangers! Who were looking at him with such curiosity, Cody above all, that he'd little alternative but to press on. 'I don't often tell people this. At most I might say that I kind of like to write. That isn't so hard. But to confess how desperately. That's another thing.' He took a deep breath. 'Especially since I must also admit to not being published. Properly, I mean. Oh, I've placed a few small pieces, minor stuff, here and there, over the years. But nothing substantial. Not like you need. Not like you want.' He took another sip of coffee. 'Anyway,' he went on, 'Paris. I've always been a Hemingway fan, you see. Even wrote a story once, about following in his footsteps, and the Paris years, they cast the strongest spell.' Reverently, as you might count the beads of a rosary, he listed some names. '*Les Deux Magots. Café de Flore. Brasserie Lipp. La Closerie des Lilas*. The bar at the Ritz. Shakespeare and Company. All that drink-fuelled glamour. That's the writing front for me. That's what I aspire to. And his ability of course to tell the truth. Those true, true sentences. The absolute best.'

'Heavens!' said Margaret. 'The writing front! You make it sound like a war. Poor man.' Her tone was not unsympathetic.

'Paris for me,' interrupted Simon, possibly in an effort to lighten the mood, 'means Disneyland.' His eyes were on his aunt. 'I went once as a kid. With my class. You probably won't remember, Auntie M, no reason why you should, although I guess I would have sent you a card. Usually did. But anyway, we never got into the city itself, only the outskirts.'

'So would Paris be your choice too?' asked Cody.

Simon frowned. 'No, I also went on another school trip, skiing this time – you paid, Auntie M, so this you will remember – and I just loved the mountains. The snow. It was all so... clean, I guess. A lovely blank. I really liked how fresh everything seemed. Unspoilt.' He was still frowning, however, as if not entirely convinced by his own description.

'That card,' said Margaret, 'the snowy one, yes, of course. I remember that card especially. Still have it indeed. But then I have all your cards. Every single one.'

'So for me,' said Simon, frown still in place, 'the Alps. That would be my first choice. And before the glaciers all melt too.'

'And you Margaret?' Cody had transferred his gaze to their only female. 'Your wish? Your desire?'

'Rome.' She said it without hesitation; no pause; no frown; the barest, simplest statement of fact. Turning from Simon to Cody she repeated: 'For me, it would have to be Rome.'

'You've been before? Or just because...'

'Yes, on an art trip once, if you must know, although it was all a very long time ago, another life almost...' She tailed off.

'Sorry,' said Cody, looking again at each of them in turn. 'None of this is meant to put you on the spot. All I require is that you remain open. That you trust me with your hopes. Which are so various! You've mentioned such different places. Paris.

The Alps. Rome. You couldn't get more different! And isn't that the amazing thing about Europe? It's full of variety. Almost anything is possible. You just have to be receptive.' He tapped his watch. 'But if we sit here all day, we won't achieve a thing. Rendezvous in the lobby in half an hour?'

Obediently, they began heading for the door, Geoffrey bringing up the rear. From which vantage point he saw, as they passed the buffet table, how Margaret nudged a reluctant Simon into nabbing a couple of apples, which she then slipped into her bag. He couldn't help but smile at how neatly the woman's prudence echoed Simon's earlier behaviour with the butter; although the young man's reluctance to do his aunt's bidding spoke of other things too. Meanwhile, the pretty young waitress was bent over a nearby table, clearing away the detritus of someone else's breakfast. Geoffrey darted over, not noticing that Margaret had turned at the door and was watching him quizzically.

'Thank you,' said Geoffrey, touching her on the arm, 'for the *zahăr*. And have a good day! You looked after us very well. I wanted you to know that.'

***

Re-entering the lobby half an hour later, Margaret discovered that Geoffrey, whom she wouldn't have expected to be punctual, was in fact ahead of her, sitting on a couch against the wall, his leather bag on his lap, also an open notebook, in which he was scribbling. She paused in her advance across the gleaming marble floor, wondering what exactly to make of him. She knew from experience that for men who'd once been lucky in the looks department – as Geoffrey so manifestly had – the fading of handsomeness seldom proved much of a brake. Often the reverse. Look at the way he'd hit on that poor waitress when leaving the breakfast room! But then you had also to consider how he'd spoken about wanting to write. How flayed he'd looked. How vulnerable. Which told another tale.

'No sign of the others?' she asked, coming to a halt before him.

He looked up with a start, snapping his notebook shut as he did so.

'No, not yet.'

'Do you mind?' She indicated the couch.

'Be my guest.' He stowed away the notebook.

They sat in silence to begin with, each sharply aware of the other, yet unable to find words.

Until eventually she said: 'Was it a flyer?'

'Was what a flyer?'

'That alerted you to this trip.'

He nodded.

'Put through the door?'

'Put through the door.'

'Quite unexpectedly? All on its own?'

Again he nodded.

'For me as well. And so few details, just that stuff about trust and the allure of mystery and how when people ask too many questions it can sometimes be a form of cowardice.'

'Like a sort of dare. Not your usual kind of tourist bumpf at all.'

'Yet I rang the number and you did too, you must have, if you're also here.'

'Guilty as charged!'

'And then just as suddenly it starts, without us even realising.'

'Like a sort of dream.'

'Yet we're obviously awake.' Then she said: 'So I've been thinking.'

'Yes?'

'And you know what it reminds me of? There's an old play by J.M. Barrie that my godfather really liked and would talk about. You won't know it, I'm sure, or I'd be surprised if you did, since it's not well known, unlike *Peter Pan*.'

'Aha! The boy who couldn't grow up.'

'Wouldn't, I think you'll find. But anyway, this other play, I can't now recall the title, but it's about this funny old man who invites a group of people to stay with him on midsummer night. A forest grows in his garden that wasn't there before. The forest of the second chance is what it is and when the guests walk into it, which they all do, one by one, they really can't help themselves, they're insanely curious, just like we are – well! They all get to live alternative lives. The lives they've always dreamed of.'

'Wow!'

'Though they do all come back in the end, I hasten to add. To the house, that is. The forest's only temporary.'

'And this forest teaches them – what? I'm guessing there must be a moral.'

'In essence, they learn that you always carry yourself with you. There are no magic solutions. Even in the forest, they're still the same people. *Dear Brutus!*' She let out a cry. 'That's it! The title! As in the lines from Shakespeare.'

'I see.'

'And the solutions they thought they wanted for themselves don't always work either. Though there is one very moving scene where one of the characters, he's a painter, gets to meet the daughter he never had. She's new.'

Her voice suddenly cracked and he wondered for a moment whether she might be about to cry. But with a quick little shrug she continued: 'Anyway, the man in the play, the host, is very old, maybe hundreds of years, so I'm not suggesting it's completely parallel, yet there's something about Cody that – well, as I was brushing my teeth just now, Cody made me think of him, that's all.'

'Wow!' repeated Geoffrey.

'There's so much that isn't clear,' sighed Margaret. 'But if we ask too many questions...'

'I know, I know.'

'Like if we've only just decided on the Anne Frank house, how is it that Cody apparently has tickets? It must book out weeks in advance, that sort of place. Unless he has prior knowledge? But how can he? Unless...'

'Unless,' said Geoffrey, 'as you seem to be suggesting, magic is somehow involved.'

Whereupon Cody materialised in front of them. Or rather, he must have walked across the lobby while they were speculating about the trip and they only noticed when he was within a few feet of their couch. A red cap was jammed jauntily onto his blond hair and he'd a rolled umbrella in his right hand. Presumably to hold up so they could more easily see and follow him as they went around the city, since he'd said the day would be fine and there'd been no prospect of rain that Margaret had noticed on her walk to and from the church.

In every respect, then, your ordinary, average, run-of-the-mill holiday guide at the start of his working day. No sign, none at all, of magic.

Margaret and Geoffrey exchanged a glancing look, in which there was tacit agreement not to ask any leading questions for the time being.

'No Simon?' queried Cody. 'Because we should really get going.'

'I'm afraid,' said Margaret, 'that when it comes to time-keeping, Simon can't always be relied upon. Youth! I fear we might find ourselves waiting on him quite a bit in the course of the coming week.'

Then the elevator pinged, its doors slid open and there he was, the latecomer, squashed in among a chattering Chinese family, who expanded noisily across the lobby, carrying Simon with them in their surge towards the hotel's revolving door.

'Shall we?' asked Cody of the others.

As he began shepherding Margaret and Geoffrey in the same direction, Simon stopped just short of the door in order to stare fascinatedly – or so it appeared – at the sizeable coat-stand to the right of it. A number of garments hung there, including a dark blue raincoat, which Simon now reached for and fleetingly touched. Then he did the oddest thing. He grabbed another coat and hung it over the one he'd just fingered.

'Really, Simon!' Margaret was chiding in the interim. 'Must you always be so slipshod when it comes to being on time?'

'Sorry!' Simon swung round guiltily. 'Did I keep you?'

'But we're all here now,' said Cody consolingly, 'that's the main thing. After you!'

Obedient to the last, his charges trooped outside ahead of him, allowing their guide the opportunity to scan the coat-stand for himself. What was it exactly, he wondered, that had attracted Simon to a random garment? And why on earth did he himself feel as though he might be implicated? Not only that, but why, despite his need to be concentrating on the task at hand, to be thinking only of the others, never himself, why did this possibility occasion a flicker of obscure excitement? It was all most strange, even for a person for whom strangeness was their stock in trade.

***

As Margaret had suspected, there was a substantial queue outside the Anne Frank house and you needed a timed ticket (which Cody did have) to enter. But that the secret annex, where the two families and Fritz Pfeffer had hidden, should turn out to be a series of empty rooms, through which they were all slowly and claustrophobically funnelled, this she hadn't anticipated. Some sort of re-creation was what she'd been expecting. For the rooms to look exactly as they'd originally been, in every detail, not just what was on the walls.

In a low voice, Cody explained how the Nazis had stripped the annex bare and how Otto Frank, the only member of the group to survive the holocaust, had then insisted that it remain so. How better, Otto had said, to symbolise the decimation?

'And that it does of course,' said Margaret afterwards, standing with Geoffrey in the middle of the shop. 'Most powerfully. Although I do feel I might have known beforehand. Paid more attention, I suppose. That's how that annex makes me feel. Like I should have paid attention.'

'What chastens me,' said Geoffrey, 'is being brought back to earth by all of this.' He gestured at the surrounding cardboard models of the annex, the jigsaw puzzles, the tote bags, the T-shirts. 'Must we always monetise everything?'

A girl of about Anne Frank's age was standing before a specially boxed edition of the diary, deciding perhaps whether or not she could afford to buy one. It did look expensive. Until Simon, who was nearer the girl, stepped closer, having also noticed what Geoffrey just had: that her shoulders were heaving and she was crying.

'Are you all right?' asked Simon. 'Is there anything I can...?'

'Here!' instructed Margaret. 'Give her this.' She handed Simon a lace handkerchief.

From Geoffrey's perspective, the tableau thus formed – distressed adolescent, concerned young man, helpful older woman – rather negated what Margaret had said about not paying enough attention. Or his own dismissal of the shop, come to that. The boxed edition wasn't something the crying girl wished to buy. It was something she wished to escape. Something she wished did not exist, and not just in a merchandising sense. Yet exist it did, as did all of the past, every second of it, waiting with dreadful patience on those moments when it could rip aside the present and make itself felt again.

'That's right,' murmured Isobel in his ear. 'Think your lofty thoughts. See where they get you.'

'Are we done here, do you imagine?' asked Cody in Geoffrey's other ear. 'I was thinking we could perhaps walk into the Jordaan and find a café for lunch. It's a nice area and afterwards the Rijksmuseum's not far.'

'Poor girl,' said Margaret, joining them. 'She's very upset. But then I was too, at the same age, which was also when I picked up the diary and read it. The thought that it could have been you, so then of course you wonder just how you would have coped. If at all.'

'I told her,' said Simon, who'd also joined them, 'that she can keep the handkerchief. Hope that's okay, Auntie M?'

Geoffrey cleared his throat. 'Cody's proposing,' he said, 'that we go into the Jordaan and find ourselves somewhere for lunch. Before the Rijksmuseum and your *Jewish Bride*, Margaret, which I hope won't suggest the same sort of history as we've been witness to here. I'm not sure I could stand it if so. All very well, Cody, to celebrate Europe for being so full of variety, which it undoubtedly is, but when you say that almost anything is possible...' His brow furrowed. 'There are two sides to that coin.'

'Well, actually,' said Margaret, 'the name is perhaps a misnomer. If I remember right, it's only called *The Jewish Bride* because some nineteenth-century art collector thought it depicted a Jewish father giving his daughter a necklace as a wedding gift. When actually the painting is more obviously of a couple in love. Dressed as the biblical couple Isaac and Rebecca, that's the general consensus. Although no one knows for sure. But anyway, it's their love that's important. Love not hate. That's what Rembrandt wanted to capture. The nature of love.'

'So let's not dawdle then,' said Cody. 'After this morning, a little love can't go amiss. Can it now?'

Outside, they walked along Prinsengracht, admiring the handsome brick buildings with their lavishly windowed gables, above which, as Cody pointed out, you could still see the means by which the householders would winch up whatever needed taking inside. A tourist boat glided by, in which the skipper was also drawing the attention of his passengers to the houses and their architecture, their windows and their winches. Then they headed into the heart of the Jordaan, stopping for lunch at a café that had tables on the pavement in the sun.

By contrast, although it did allow for outside light, the Rijksmuseum was suitably dim and their pace slowed as they went in a respectful hush from painting to painting. The Rembrandts they found in the gallery of honour, heart of the museum's collection. Simon and Cody immediately made for the enormous highlight on the far wall, while Margaret turned into the side alcove that contained what she was after, with Geoffrey following. Here they stood side by side, absorbing the painting's every brushstroke. The way the man leaned protectively towards the woman, one hand placed upon her breast. The way her smaller hand brushed his, a feather's touch. The fact that neither of them was looking at the other, nor at the viewer, which made their intimacy all the more telling. The glow of golden light on the man's voluminous sleeve. Her ruddy cheeks and the corresponding hue of her dress. Tenderness and absorption.

'They say it reduced van Gogh to tears,' said Margaret. 'He wrote to his brother Theo, you know, to the effect that one must have died many times to paint like this.'

Geoffrey gave utterance to a further: 'Wow!'

'He also said he'd give up ten years of his life just to sit for two weeks staring at it, with only a crust of stale bread to eat.'

'What an earful!' muttered Geoffrey. 'And from a man I usually think of as rather lacking in the ear department!'

Margaret looked at him witheringly. 'Is everything a joke to you?'

'Of course not!'

'What then? Why?' Her gaze was challenging.

'I guess I get embarrassed,' said Geoffrey at last. 'By too much emotion.'

'Yet you want to write?' Margaret's gaze did not let up.

'Maybe,' replied Geoffrey, reaching for another thought, 'that's going to be the point of this highly unusual and mysterious week. That we say things, do things, learn things, that normally we wouldn't. Like in that old play your godfather liked.'

'Second chances,' said Margaret quietly, returning her attention to the painting. 'Wouldn't it be nice to think so.' She smiled sadly. 'But come! Let's leave this couple to themselves and find the others.'

Afterwards, they strolled along Singel, past the Vondelpark, to the Leidseplein, where they sat outside again and ordered drinks: foaming beers for Simon and Geoffrey, a coffee for Margaret and a mineral water for Cody.

'I must say, you've managed to set a very pleasant pace,' said Margaret to their guide after their drinks had arrived. 'I've enjoyed today.'

'Me too,' agreed Simon. 'Awesome, just awesome.'

'Even though you're stuck with us oldies?' teased his aunt.

'Cody's not so old. And anyway, in this city, there are young people everywhere.'

'Unsurprisingly,' said Geoffrey. 'It's a cool place to visit. On a human scale and you also have the water. Hard to beat.' He raised his glass. 'Thank you, Cody! You've started us off well. My appetite is whetted.'

'Just so!' echoed Margaret, although she did not go so far as to raise her glass.

Their guide smiled.

Then they returned to the hotel for a rest before dinner, where, as Cody couldn't help noticing after they'd passed through the revolving door, Simon looked immediately at the coat-stand. The coats and hats that had been there previously had mostly gone. Not so, however, the dark blue raincoat; that remained very much in evidence.

Day 2

Simon escaped the grip of his dream to find himself in much fancier surroundings than those he'd gone to sleep in after their evening meal in Amsterdam. They'd eaten in a cosy, pub-like restaurant serving mainly steaks, then a nightcap in an equally cosy brown café and a relatively early night since everyone had agreed that after everything the day had thrown at them, to stay out late would be a step too far. And indeed, Simon had fallen asleep immediately. To be woken by, of all things, a cuckoo.

The cuckoo was housed in an ornately carved little wooden chalet affixed to the wall opposite the bed and its piping call was underscored by a chime. There was one call for every such chime and Simon thought he counted seven in all. Coming upright, he discovered that although some plum-coloured curtains were holding back the morning light, it was still possible to distinguish the room's principal features. Namely, that the painting alongside the cuckoo clock was of mountains; that the chest of drawers below it was also ornately carved. He took in the gleam of brass fittings; a wingback chair; a substantial cupboard of the sort that might well have contained the entrance to Narnia (the books had been particular favourites of his as a child) and a wide door, half open, through which he could see a section of richly tiled bathroom.

On waking in Amsterdam, although he had of course puzzled over how you could fall asleep in one place only to open your eyes in another, the day had held so many surprises (like the raincoat near the hotel door) that, by the end of it, he'd given up asking. Nor had Cody, who could be quite steely when he chose, encouraged too much in the way of introspection about the mechanics of their trip. How had their guide put it? Uncertainty was part of the journey. They needed to give themselves over to it. Go with the flow. Rather like the Narnia cupboard. You didn't question why or how a cupboard could house another world. You just accepted that it did.

Briefly, Simon flirted with the idea of opening the cupboard to find out whether it did in fact lead anywhere. Except that what lay beyond the heavy curtains was ultimately more spellbinding and so this was where he now went, to see if the painting and the cuckoo clock provided accurate clues.

Both did. A valley that was partly pasture, partly wood, dotted here and there with red roofs, fell away in gradations of enticing green to rise again in the distance as a trio of snowy mountains, whitely etched against the bluest of skies. So! He was in the Alps, which was where he'd said he'd like to be. (*They* were in the driving seat. *They* were the nucleus.) Although as obviously – it being summer – this wasn't a winter wonderland.

But did this in any way stay the memories? Not in the slightest.

He was on tiptoe at another window, smaller, set higher in the wall, in the cluttered dormitory he'd shared with his classmates, looking out purely on snow, snow everywhere, the whole world blanketed by a thick white weight. With Richard, his best friend, alongside him, equally amazed.

'Hey,' Richard had whispered, not wanting anyone else to hear. 'Let's sneak out before supper. Just the two of us, okay. Horseface won't notice. What do you say?'

Simon had said yes. Of course he'd said yes. He always acquiesced to Richard, no matter what. He'd have put his hand in the fire for Richard.

'I'll go first,' said his best friend, who invariably took the lead. 'And try not to look so guilty, hey. Or you'll give the game away.'

For the young Simon, it had been like stepping – literally stepping – into Narnia: his first experience of a world outside the norm; everything an unexpected white, dazzling, homogenous and clean, which instantly gave him permission to run free with Richard along the pristine pavement and into a small park, where they'd pelted each other with snowballs and Richard had chased him round in ever decreasing circles until Simon had at last allowed his friend to corner him and hadn't minded in the least when Richard had thrown himself on top of Simon, pressing down with all his weight. A moment that Simon would never forget.

He went smartly into the bathroom to run himself a bath, where he found the old-fashioned tub to be very large and good no doubt for soaking your aching muscles in after a day's skiing or a long summer hike. But if he thought it could also soak away memories, he was very much mistaken and, as he lay in the hot water, he also remembered how, after their eyes had locked and they'd smiled at each other, Richard had roughly rolled off him with the words: 'Why the fuck are you looking at me like that? Don't be so creepy.'

'What do you mean?'

'It's disgusting.'

'What's disgusting?'

'You are.'

And so the moment had ended and for the rest of that skiing week his one-time best friend had steered clear of him. Back at school too, where Richard had become even more distant and unfriendly until, finally, he'd actively turned on Simon and started to tease him publicly for being, as he liked to term it, such a sissy.

Simon reached for the soap and started to lather himself. All very well to wish for the Alps, he was thinking, but don't imagine the good can ever be separated from the bad. Or was that the point perhaps? For him to confront them both. In equal measure.

***

Cody's thoughts that second morning, as he sat doing some paperwork at the desk in his room by the window, were also existential. He too was questioning himself. Wondering what exactly he was after and whether, by having continually to concentrate on the needs of others, he wasn't by definition paying insufficient attention to his own.

His window overlooked the hotel car park: SUVs and Sports Sedans, Hatchbacks and Jeeps, a few natty sports cars. By and large, the hotel's guests looked to be fairly wealthy; the sort who would also expect their rooms to have superior views to his. It was only life's enablers and guides, staff of whatever description, who got put at the rear. And with this notion came an uncharacteristic burst of self pity. Did he really want to be tucked away forever? How about enjoying the superior view for a change? After so many years at the coalface.

He'd been in his gap year, on the last leg of a fairly standard, box-ticking trip around the world: India, South-East Asia, Australia, New Zealand, South America, the States and Canada. (Africa he was saving for later. Europe too, since it was on his doorstep.) He was down to the last of his money, eating only once a day when, after a very scant meal in a café in downtown Toronto, the old man had approached him.

'You look hungry still,' the old-timer had said. 'Let me buy you some dessert.'

Being (as he knew) good-looking, Cody was no stranger to overtures of this sort and quite naturally viewed them with suspicion. But this old man appeared different. There was something otherworldly about him, utterly removed from fleshly concerns.

'That's very good of you,' he heard himself saying. 'Thank you. Why not?'

The old man waved for a waitress to bring back the menu. 'I'm struck,' he said, 'by how well you travel. Calm. You're awfully calm. I've also seen how you notice things. How quick you are to explore. How sensitive to your surroundings. Good antennae.'

Now here *was* something to raise suspicion: the fact that a total stranger had apparently been watching his every move. Over quite a period of time too, by the sound of it. Although how could that be possible? Cody had only been in Toronto a couple of days. Unless...?

He looked questioningly at the old man, whose deep green eyes were both striking and piercing. Then he said meekly: 'Go on, please.'

Later, he would learn the eye trick himself. How to stare a person down. In fact, it was one of his very first lessons in the job. But at the time, he thought merely how nice that someone should be bothering with him in this way.

'I have a hunch,' the old man continued as a famished Cody started in on the pudding he'd ordered; tart and ice-cream; he could still remember the taste of it, 'that you might be just the sort of person I'm after. Allow me to explain...'

On that occasion, he'd only told Cody the bare minimum; but he'd said enough to intrigue his listener, who'd spent much of his round-the-world trip wondering what he might do after obtaining a planned degree in social anthropology. He knew he wanted to work with people, but in what capacity? Until Cedric – for that was the old man's name – had provided a possible answer by coming to sit at his table in a downtown Toronto café and fix him with a pair of piercing eyes the same colour as his own.

At the meal's end, Cody had happily taken Cedric's card and, on the flight home, decided to call the number on it just as soon as he landed. There'd been no reply, however, despite quite a few attempts, and in the end he'd put the card away and more or less forgotten about it. He'd obtained his degree, found a first job, then a second, and it was only when clearing out some drawers a few years later that he'd come across the card again, tucked between some brochures. His first impulse had been to throw it away. That funny old man in that downtown café: it was as if he'd dreamed the whole episode. But some instinct made him try the number anyway – and this time his call had been answered.

'Ah-ha!' Cedric's reedy voice sounded delighted. 'Ready at last! Now how are you placed this coming Saturday? Shall we say midday-ish? I'll come to you.'

There had followed fifteen largely contented years. The chance to travel more widely than he'd ever have thought possible. To be of real service to others. To help them make connections they might not otherwise have made. See themselves more clearly. Bring about change. What wasn't there to like for someone of Cody's gifts and disposition?

But – and it was a big BUT – lately the job had begun to chafe. Serving others was all very well, but – again that BUT – always being at someone else's beck and call was leading him to wonder where and how *he* figured in the pattern woven by every journey. Was his view always to be of the utter arse-end of things?

***

Margaret and Geoffrey were on the terrace in the sun, cups of leisurely post-breakfast coffee to hand, listening to the hotel's Swiss proprietor explain about the Chinese. The proprietor's name was Bruno and the hotel had been in his family for three generations, he said. In the past, it had catered almost exclusively to small family groups. Or couples. Sometimes singles. Mainly from Europe, although people had also come from other parts. But never like now, with the Chinese, who were present in unbelievable numbers.

This conversation had been triggered by Margaret noticing the many suitcases in the lobby as she'd walked through it on her way to join Geoffrey, who was there before her, at a table on the far edge of the sun-drenched terrace on which breakfast was being served. About fifty cases in total, she reckoned. Maybe more.

'Why such a quantity?' she asked Bruno as he stopped by their table later to enquire whether or not they'd enjoyed their meal. 'Who can they all belong to?'

The proprietor spread his hands. 'This is a new thing happening,' he said, the trace of an accent giving his words an extrinsic gloss. 'In the sixties and beginning seventies, it was of course the Americans. They were the people who travelled much. Europe was new for them, you understand, of Europe they couldn't get enough. There's a film from that time: *If It's Tuesday, This Must Be Belgium*. About Americans on a – how do you say? – a whistling stop tour. Belgium today, another country tomorrow, etcetera, etcetera. *Vite, vite*. A comedy. Now of course the Americans have grown up. Europe isn't so strange for them. They visit in a different way. More slow, agreeable. They take their time, not all in a week. But for the Chinese, everything, it's still so new. They want to see it all. So this group now, they arrive last night from Paris, today they go to the Jungfrau, they look at the glacier, they have lunch, they come down again, they take their cases from the lobby and tonight they fly – *vite, vite* – to Rome. Then, I don't know, Athens maybe. Istanbul. And after a week, they go home. One day in one place. Two maximum. And so it will go until everyone, all, have done this and they can relax, come back more slowly. Like the Americans. It's the tourist cycle.'

Margaret glanced at Geoffrey. 'Us too, it would appear,' she said wryly. 'Same sort of whirlwind routine, thanks to Cody.'

'But where were all these hordes at breakfast?' asked Geoffrey. 'I saw no sign of them.'

'Ah, so we put our big groups at the back,' explained Bruno. 'In a separate room. Not here on the terrace. The terrace would get too crowded. Also, they don't have time, not like you, to sit slowly and enjoy the view.'

'Well, it's certainly very lovely,' said Margaret with a grateful smile. 'Sun out, everything so peaceful, birdsong and the cowbells.'

'But I should go,' said Bruno with an answering smile. 'Stop my own song!'

He moved deftly to the next table, leaving Geoffrey to remark sardonically: 'So no morning view then for the frantic Chinese. Poor sods.'

'There were some in yesterday's hotel as well,' said Margaret. 'Did you notice? Coming out of the lift with Simon.'

'Poor sods,' repeated Geoffrey. He was frowning. 'Just as the whole carbon issue is coming to a head as well. Talk about bad timing.'

'Don't!' Margaret shuddered.

'Us lot, we've been so incredibly lucky. But for your nephew, say, and his generation, well – he said it himself, yesterday, when he talked about the Alps and how they're melting.' He pointed to the view they were enjoying: the green sweep of the valley, punctuated at its end by an immensity of mountain, white-tipped and soaring. 'How much longer might we have it?'

'It felt necessary at the time though,' said Margaret. She was also frowning. 'Hindsight can be a terrible thing. Back then, to me at least, it felt entirely necessary. Travel broadens the mind. We all grew up thinking that. And were we so very wrong?' She gestured to where the elegantly attired figure of Bruno was bending over another table at the terrace's edge. In his short-sleeved shirt and fawn slacks, he looked as if he might himself be on holiday; only the alertness of his posture let slip that he was actually working. 'Must Bruno go out of business? Must the Chinese be denied? How is the problem to be dealt with?'

Geoffrey shrugged. 'I wish I knew. But hey! I'm spoiling a lovely morning. I shouldn't have opened my mouth.'

'No need to apologise,' said Margaret. 'You're quite right. It's...'

'A hard nut to crack.'

'To put it mildly.'

'And if your nephew, thinking of him again, hadn't gone on a school skiing trip,' continued Geoffrey, 'by all accounts we wouldn't be here now. So it ain't all bad.' Although his saying this didn't cause Margaret to look any the happier.

'There'd been tensions at home,' she said suddenly, gazing towards the mountains. 'That's really why I treated him. So he could be away for a while. I thought he maybe needed it. But when he got back, or not long afterwards, that's when it all happened. Sorry!' She looked directly at Geoffrey, thus allowing him to see the pain in her eyes. 'I hardly know you. This isn't appropriate.'

'Please!' responded Geoffrey. 'I'm all ears. No joke intended.'

Margaret looked mountain-wards again. 'All right,' she said eventually. 'If you insist. It was a car accident. Susan and Henry were in an awful car accident. Killed instantly. That at least was a mercy. So of course I had to come back. That's when I took over. After Susan and Henry were both killed.'

Once more she turned to face Geoffrey and, for a long while, nothing further was said. Just the sound of a few other people having their breakfast, the occasional car in the town below, the wind in the trees and, carried on that wind, the chunky music of cowbells.

'Back, you say,' ventured her companion at last. He was finding it hard to meet Margaret's bleak gaze. 'Back from where, may one ask?'

'BA.'

'Sorry?'

'Buenos Aires. I'd been living in Buenos Aires.'

'Well, well! You have been around! And Susan and Henry? Am I to take it that...'

'My sister, my only sister,' said Margaret curtly. 'And her husband. Who still lived in Suffolk, still in the village where we grew up. Far from Argentina. Another world.'

'Ah! There you both are! Wonderful.' The interruption came from Cody, calling up to them from the road below. 'We were a little worried you might have wandered off already.'

Pleased to have an excuse – truth to tell, he was finding Margaret's distress hard to bear, never mind that her story left a great many questions unanswered, none of which he felt able to pursue under the circumstances – Geoffrey leapt up and went to lean over the balustrade. The road below was a narrow one, leading from the town and the town's station towards a cluster of outlying chalets further up the mountainside. Some determined walkers were striding along it, making way as they went past for Cody and Simon, who'd gone off together after an early breakfast to explore the town and were now standing slap bang in the middle of the road, staring up at the hotel.

'Recognise anything?' asked Margaret, joining Geoffrey at the balustrade.

Simon shook his head. 'I can't even be sure it was Wengen.'

'Well don't ask me,' said Margaret. 'Although I suppose that card you sent might give us a clue. We can check when we get back home.'

'It doesn't really matter,' said Simon. 'Because everything then was snow. All white. Very different.'

'So if we take the train up to the glacier,' said Cody, 'that's precisely what we'll get. Snow! Snow everywhere. Sound appealing? It's a spectacular ride.'

'I just need to go to the room first,' said Margaret. 'What should we bring? I'm assuming it can get quite nippy.'

'A jumper certainly,' said Cody. 'Ideally a jacket too, if you have one, and a scarf. Gloves? If you've packed any.'

'And you too, Simon!' instructed Margaret sternly. 'You know how susceptible you are to the cold.'

'I'll wait by the hotel gate,' said Cody. 'No need to rush. The trains are pretty frequent.'

He himself was only wearing what he'd had on yesterday – white T-shirt, white jeans, white sneakers – without even a red cap this morning to complement the outfit. Nor did he have his rolled umbrella with him, perhaps feeling it to be superfluous after their first day. But he was carrying a small rucksack, into which he'd no doubt stuffed any essentials, clothing-wise. It was his job, after all, to be prepared for all eventualities.

***

On the train, which chugged for a while alongside the road that skirted the hotel as it began its ascent up the side of the valley, going through pine trees, past sloping meadows, the occasional farm, sometimes a small station, with the high peaks towering always above them, Margaret concentrated less on the magnificence of the landscape than she did on memories of Simon. Simon at thirteen, to be exact, which was when most of them inevitably started.

The call had come mid-morning, just as she was wondering whether to go back to the flat for lunch or grab herself an empanada from the bar around the corner. She'd gone into the office to collect a file and found the phone to be ringing.

'Is that the *Hogar de Caritas*?' came a crackly voice. 'The children's home? Do you speak some English by any chance?'

'*Si*,' Margaret said without thinking. 'I mean yes. Of course I do. How can I help?'

'I need to talk with Margaret Thompson please.'

'This is she.'

36

Then the news. Susan and Henry. Outside Ipswich. A lorry. The caller was a village neighbour. Simon was with them and welcome to stay for as long as he needed, although they guessed that as his only aunt and nearest relative, Margaret would want...

'But of course,' said Margaret. '*Por supuesto*. The next available flight. What's your number?'

Packing up the flat had been surprisingly easy. She didn't possess all that much and although she'd always liked the place – the high ceilings, the elegant windows, the rich gleam of the dark wood floors – essentially it had remained a blank canvas, one which she hadn't known how to begin painting. Which brush to use. Which combination of colours. Or what subject. That least of all.

The children, however, the children were another matter. She only worked at the orphanage in a secretarial capacity, part-time at that – teaching English and some translating work were her staples – but even so: you couldn't be anywhere near the *Hogar de Caritas* without becoming aware of the children, their competing personalities, their complicated and often terrible histories, their fierce needs. Little Manuel, whose parents had perished in a mudslide. Gloria, whose mother had been gunned down in a fight between competing gangs. Florencia, who'd been abandoned on a doorstep and knew nothing of her parents. Or Joaquin, who did at least have an older brother, now of an age to hold down a job, but not yet able to offer Joaquin sufficient support. Manuel, Gloria, Florencia, Joaquin – they and many others all needed parenting and, as a consequence, everyone involved with the home, no matter how peripheral their role, eventually became something of the kind.

But now another child, as deprived, had need of her and so Margaret had left BA as precipitously and eagerly as once she'd flown in, eyes fixed on an even more compelling future.

She turned from the train window to look at where Simon was sitting alongside Geoffrey. His earnest face. The lines on his forehead, in advance of his years. The overall seriousness of his gaze. How solemnly he would blink. Little trace of a smile, although when he did smile, his whole face would light up and become radiant.

'Happy?' she queried. 'You did ask for the Alps.'

'Sure thing,' he replied, smile appearing. 'Absolutely.'

She remembered getting out of the taxi all those years ago, the driver having twice gone down the wrong lane, and standing at the door to the pretty pink cottage and pressing the bell with fingers that shook and how, instantaneously it seemed, the door had opened wide and there he was, hands by his side, those anxious eyes of his looking at her uncertainly.

'Aunt Margaret?'

Only after she'd nodded had he dared to lift his arms and only after she'd lifted her own in response and clutched him to her had he allowed himself to unbend a little.

'I'm so glad. Thank you.'

'What on earth are you thanking me for, silly boy?'

'You've come such a long way.'

'Further than you can imagine. But I'm here now. That's the important thing. And here is where I intend to stay.'

They came to a small station – little more than a mountainside halt – where a handful of walkers got out, their poles and backpacks and water bottles and maps in plastic pouches clearly proclaiming, if not trumpeting, the ardour of their intentions.

'That's something else,' said Cody as the doors slid shut behind them and the train started up again, 'that you can do in these mountains during the summer months. Walk. You can really walk. Although you do have to be careful. Come prepared. The weather can change in a heartbeat. You might think the day, like now, is sunny, but without warning a mist can come down, you can't see a thing, you're entirely lost!'

'Yet it all looks so gentle,' said Simon, indicating the slope of a passing meadow. 'Not at all how I remember it.' Over the noise of the train they could still hear the cowbells. There were spots too of bright colour where the summer flowers stood out against the green of the mountain grass and the sky remained the kind of blue it was hard to believe would ever turn treacherous. 'Under snow it was awesomely different. Sort of like a blank canvas.'

Funny! thought Margaret. *That phrase again.*

Simon was still looking out of the window, now at a small patch of forest, although very soon, as could be seen from the higher reaches on the other side of the valley, they would be above the tree line; exposed.

'So weird,' he said, 'being here again. There's a lot to... I don't know, process, I guess. Don't mean to sound heavy.'

'Well,' agreed Geoffrey, who hitherto had been largely silent as he took in the passing landscape and the reactions of his fellow travellers, 'when it comes to processing stuff, I suppose we're all in the same boat. Pretty much. Although I do obviously realise,' he added quickly, turning to the person by his side, 'from the little your aunt has told me, that for you it must be especially difficult.'

His aim had been to make Simon feel relaxed about any feelings of weirdness; but it didn't work out like that. On the contrary, what followed was a version of what Cody had just warned about: an abrupt and unforeseen change in the conversational weather, sun turning to mist and immediately Geoffrey had lost his bearings. Simon darted a furious look at his aunt. Margaret started to open her mouth. But Simon got in first.

'So!' he said, no trace of a smile now. 'What is it this time, Auntie M? Not going to uni? The garden centre? Alison? Which bit of how you think I'm wasting my life have you chosen to share with Geoffrey here?'

'Simon, really! I only told him about the crash.'

In the role he'd recently admitted aspiring to, that of full-on, committed writer, Geoffrey supposed he ought to have recovered his bearings by now and be welcoming this turn of events. For here was material with a capital M. Material! He'd only to listen and watch and take note and who knew where things might lead? But Geoffrey was also a peace-maker ('Don't you mean coward?' asked Isobel) and, as such, felt obliged to reach for oil rather than ink.

'Please, you mustn't blame your aunt,' he said, pouring his oil as liberally as he could on the troubled waters around him. 'She was only answering my questions. When you travel together you can't avoid a certain level of curiosity. It's only natural.' Cody, he noticed, was watching hawk-like; a silent referee. 'I'm really sorry if inadvertently I've upset you.'

To which Simon, who'd started to blush, all at once said: 'No, I'm the one who should apologise. It's being here, I don't know, it's getting to me big time. Sorry!'

'And look!' cried Cody. 'We're almost at our stop. Here's where we change for our final destination. The Top of Europe!'

The station they were chugging into was considerably larger than any of the halts along the way. Two lines converged: the one they'd travelled up on and another that came from some other valley completely. As a result, crowds of people were milling about on the platform, all presumably headed to or from the panorama above them of sheer rock and snow and ice, implacable full stop to the gentler green still surrounding them. Also prominently placed was a large, chalet-like hotel.

'Okay!' said Cody once they'd joined the crowd. 'Now we queue with that line over there for the little cogwheel train that will take us to the viewing point on the edge of the glacier. Where, weather permitting, which today it's bound to, I think, you can even walk out onto the ice. There's also a sort of ice palace inside the building – well, under the glacier, in point of fact – a couple of cafés and lots and lots of meteorological information and displays and stuff.'

'Don't you ever get tired,' asked Geoffrey, 'of coming to these places and having to say and, worse, do the same thing over and over? I know I would! And I'm a blasted teacher!'

'Actually,' replied Cody, leading them towards where they needed to be, 'this is one spot I haven't visited before. Unusually for me.'

'Really? Yet you appear to know all about it!'

'Homework.' Cody's smile was offhand, as if the subject were of little significance. 'But now we really must concentrate on finding ourselves seats. On the right ideally, that's where you get the best views. This little train can get very crowded, or so I've read.'

He wasn't exaggerating. The queue for it was long and there was a limited number of carriages and, in the end, only Margaret and Geoffrey managed to sit; Simon and Cody were left standing. Still, the view as they started up the rock face promised to be unprecedented and after they'd entered a long tunnel they all had to get out anyway so as to look through some large windows that had been skillfully cut into the rock overlooking a sea of ice.

'The Aletsch glacier,' explained Cody. 'Or part of it. There's more to come.'

At the very top – the so-called Top of Europe; although, as Cody also pointed out, technically it wasn't quite that – they crammed into an elevator that whisked them to an observation deck and more of the glacier; snow and ice on every side; another world altogether.

'Yup!' said Simon. '*This* is what I remember.' He turned to Margaret. 'Sorry I was so rude earlier. Didn't mean to be. Just jittery.' He laid an apologetic hand on her arm before also looking at Geoffrey. 'I hope you can both understand?'

'Of course,' said Geoffrey. 'No explanation needed.'

'And aren't we all glad,' added Margaret, 'that Cody made us bring warm things!'

It had been hot on the hotel terrace. Up here, however, on the wide walkway they'd stepped out onto that ran around the building, the cold was biting. Just as well, therefore – Margaret was right – that Cody had issued those instructions. Though what she didn't mention was how strange it had been to find, on going to her room, that she'd packed herself a warm jacket and a scarf and some gloves. She didn't remember putting these items aside when she'd got down her case to fill it. Oh, yes! This trip was brimful of surprises all right! And, as amazingly, Simon had also come prepared – no nagging needed for once – since he was also possessed of a jacket and gloves. Only Geoffrey had been caught short. Just a pullover, that's all the poor man had, and already he was shivering.

'You look cold,' said Margaret. 'Shall we go inside?'

'If no one minds,' said Simon, 'I'll join the others on the ice for a bit.' He pointed to where splashes of colour, in the form of other day trippers, contrasted vividly with the surrounding white in a visual echo of how, lower down, the summer flowers had stood out against the green of the meadows. Although these splashes of colour were on the move as the day trippers had their photographs taken with the Swiss flag that was flying there, or threw snowballs at each other, or simply tramped about, gawping.

'You'll find at least one café on the floors below,' said Cody to Margaret. 'Also a couple of restaurants. Then the ice palace, of course. Not to be missed. And the various displays.'

'Plus a shop or two, no doubt,' said Geoffrey. 'There's always a shop.'

'Do be careful now!' Margaret's focus was on Simon. 'No straying from the path. Don't want you coming to any harm.'

'Oh, do stop worrying, Auntie M! Really. I know how to handle myself.'

'So is it all right, then, if I leave everyone to their own devices for a bit?' asked Cody. 'As I say, there's really no shortage of attractions.'

Nor was there. The building comprised a bewilderment of lower floors, containing all that Cody had promised. Even a Lindt Chocolate Heaven. Not that Margaret and Geoffrey were much tempted by any of this. Instead, after availing themselves of the toilets, they headed for the café, where they nabbed a table and Geoffrey did the honours ordering-wise. Two coffees and some strudel. That they had found tempting.

'I'm afraid,' said Margaret after an initial bite, 'that I rather irritate him.'

'Your nephew, is this?'

'I just can't seem to get it right these days.'

'Who can, with the young? And if you don't mind me saying, he does seem... well, rather troubled. That unexpected outburst on the train. Quite violent, wasn't it?'

The attentiveness of Geoffrey's gaze as he regarded Margaret with a cocked head over the rim of his cup, together with the way his heavy glasses magnified his gaze, meant that before she knew it, Margaret was filling in the background. Almost as if she were at confession. Although there were, of course, a great many things she chose not to share with this decidedly secular version of a priest.

'We live in quite a small village,' was how she began, 'and Simon's very bright and I suppose I always expected him to want to get out. Stretch his wings, as most young people do. But in his last few years of school he got himself a weekend job at a local garden centre and that's where he's opted to stay. No thought of university, although he could have gone easily. Should have, in my opinion. Like I say, he's very bright. It's such a waste. But something holds him back.'

'It's not enough to just like plants?'

'Oh, don't get me wrong, he's terrifically good at what he does. Malcolm, who runs the nursery, speaks very highly of him. And it isn't only the plants. Simon's good with people too, terribly good. Malcolm doesn't ever want to let him go, he says. Which is perhaps part of the problem. And then there's Alison of course.'

'Alison?'

'But I should stop! This really is too much to be burdening you with.'

'No, please! Go on! I'm fascinated.' Geoffrey's lenses caught the light in morse-coded flashes of encouragement.

Margaret swallowed. 'So when Susan and Henry were killed, the neighbours who took him in, they did so because Simon and their daughter, that's Alison, were really close. He was always round at their place, like they were a second family. Sort of.' She faltered, a look coming into her eyes of such sadness, such desolation, that Geoffrey wondered whether he should order her to stop. But she was continuing anyway. 'The church played its part.'

'The church? Really? How?'

'Sorry, I know this is a lot to take in and I'm not explaining it very well.'

'You're doing just fine.'

'My sister was a born again Christian, you see. She and Henry both, he introduced her, and it was, is, very tight knit, their church community. Very intense. All consuming. And so were Alison's parents. Born again, I mean. Evangelical. However you say it. That's what initially brought the two families together.'

'And you're not, I take it? Born again?'

Margaret shook her head. 'Heavens, no! I have my faith, certainly, but it's of a very different order. Horse of *quite* another colour and I'm afraid Susan and I really didn't see eye to eye on that score. Though of course I was ultimately glad that the church provided them with friends. Someone for Simon to turn to. They're very kind at heart, Alison's parents. Alison as well, she's lovely, really lovely, and I always imagined that she and Simon might one day...' She let the sentence dangle, having something more pressing to add. 'Alison's a free thinker, you see, she's broken completely with her parents' church and then she helped me when I made Simon question things too, which he'd been doing anyway, even before the accident. Oh, it's all so complicated. But the main thing is, she and Simon, Alison and Simon, they're awfully close, you've only to look at the pair of them to appreciate how good they are together. A real team. She provides encouragement and I could...'

'You,' said Geoffrey, finishing the sentence for her, 'could stop worrying yourself.'

'Precisely! Because you're absolutely right, I do. I worry terribly. The poor boy seems... I hesitate to say this, but to me he seems not only troubled, but actually lost.' Her eyes appeared sadder and more desolate than ever. 'There! I've said it. Unless it's even worse, of course, and it's just that he's lost as far as I'm concerned.'

To this final remark, there was no easy answer, nor did Geoffrey attempt one. Rather, he let the silence settle while, with his fork, he lifted the last of the strudel to his lips.

'If it's any help,' he said eventually, 'it's taken me my whole life and still I haven't found myself. Sometimes these things require time. And maybe, just maybe, they're the better for it. You know what they say. Easy come, easy go.'

'Sorry!' said Margaret, who'd been blowing her nose. 'Here I am banging on about me and poor Simon as if we're the only ones who matter. How rude! I've hardly asked you anything about yourself.'

Geoffrey felt emboldened by this to reach across the table and pat Margaret on the wrist. Just lightly. He knew better than to let his fingers linger.

'Divorced, if you must know,' he said, deciding to ignore how quickly Margaret had retracted her hand. 'Two whole years now. She went off with a good friend of ours. Originally a lodger from when we had our first flat. Lodger with benefits, as I discovered later. Like in a really bad novel, which in part, the early part, it did also become once. Ironically.'

'And your ex is...?'

'Isobel? An economist. Quite high flying.'

'And you're a teacher, yes?'

Geoffrey nodded. 'Geography. Quite low flying. Though right now, I'm on sabbatical.'

'Aha!' cried Margaret. 'So that's where the writing comes in! You want a proper shot at it. Of course! As you were explaining yesterday. How wonderful.'

It would never have occurred to Geoffrey to state it quite so baldly; or so positively. But she was not wrong. Hence the journal. Hence a whole lot of things he hardly dared articulate. And because this was so and he wished to stay on the safe side, what he did now was place his cup and saucer neatly on his empty plate and look at his watch and say: 'But enough about me! How long, do you think, will Simon take on the ice? Shall we push on? Avoiding Lindt Heaven if we possibly can.' He pinched his stomach. 'Following that strudel, I fear Lindt Heaven would actually be a touch hellish.'

***

After the others had gone back inside, Simon made another circuit of the walkway that ran around the building. The views really were astonishing. Coming up on the train, the world had been a gentle one. Calming green meadows on every side; the cows with their bells; the many trees; the summer flowers. Picture postcard perfect – like what he would have sent his parents and/or Auntie M had he been visiting at this time of year as a young boy.

Up here it was different. Only rock, snow and ice; scudding clouds; a few quite ominous-looking blackbirds who'd come to perch on the railings in the hope of being fed by the visitors; and a larger scattering of people on the glacier itself, revelling in the titanic contrast between worlds.

Simon's urge to join those on the glacier became overpowering and the next thing he knew, he was looking back at the building on whose observation deck he'd been standing, trying to work out where exactly on the ice he now was. From above, it had been relatively easy to distinguish north from south, east from west. Down below, however, with everything so white, less so. Although the mountain peaks did help and he also remembered noticing a purple anorak with yellow stripes in the area where he'd wanted to be. Now he saw the anorak again, some ten metres to his right, so began trudging in that direction.

Which of them spoke first? Afterwards, he couldn't be sure. He just knew that as he neared the anorak, he'd started to feel dizzy. Then he'd heard his name being called and Richard was smiling down at him in much the way he'd smiled when lying on top of Simon in that park, before abruptly rolling off and leaving Simon to get back up by himself.

'Are you all right? Here, mate, let me give you a hand. Easy does it!'

This older Richard was more solicitous. He made sure Simon was on his feet again before stepping back.

'Amazing!' he said. 'What are the chances? Here of all places and after so many years. Is that what made you fall? The shock of seeing me again? Or the sheer pleasure?' And when Simon, who was in the act of brushing the snow from himself, didn't reply: 'On our own, are we? No Alison?'

They stared at each other in continuing disbelief. *How long do I want for this to last?* Simon asked himself. *If I am, as Cody says, in the driving seat.*

'No, no Alison,' he confirmed. 'You're right. On my own.'

'What?' demanded Richard next. 'Why are you still looking at me in that creepy fashion?'

'I suppose,' said Simon slowly, 'I have some questions. Just a few.'

He was remembering the overall shape of their first proper encounter. Richard in the playground at school, in a smirking huddle with Chris Topham after the two of them had been called up before the whole class by Horseface because their essays had been 'rather too similar'. Horseface being someone you didn't trifle with. Yet Richard and Chris Topham had seemed totally unfazed. As if they'd somehow got the better of their teacher, rather than it being the other way around.

What else had he been drawn to, apart from Richard's cockiness and compactness of body? Nothing really, but that was enough and shortly afterwards, again in the playground, the two of them had finally spoken. After another of Horseface's lessons, in which Simon had been singled out for the excellence of his own homework.

'So I guess you weren't watching the footie last night?' Richard had said tauntingly; but a bit in admiration too. 'Like everyone else who didn't get such high bloody marks.'

'You say I'm always the one,' said Simon now, to the older Richard, as it hit home. 'You say I always look at you, whereas actually, actually – you were the one to speak first. I'd forgotten that.'

'Was I?'

'You know you were. So my question is: why?'

Richard appeared nettled. Then he said: 'You looked lonely.'

'You felt sorry for me?'

'Is that so hard to believe?'

'I wasn't just someone else whose homework you wanted to copy? And anyway, if you're so considerate, how come, after that skiing trip, you started to avoid me? And Alison? The thing with Alison. Explain that if you dare!'

Despite his accustomed air of superiority, Richard was looking ever more uncomfortable. And in that instant, having asked his questions, it dawned on Simon that the answers were, in the final analysis, irrelevant. The crucial thing was not why Richard had first spoken to him, or pulled away in that park, or any of the stuff coming afterwards; what mattered was that, in so doing, he'd opened Simon's eyes to what lay coiled within. The stirrings of his sexual self. That's what Simon now realised from being in Richard's company again. His own agency. And the ironic fact that perhaps he ought, if anything, to be thanking Richard.

Though because he also now wanted for the encounter to be over – it had served its purpose – all he said was: 'On second thoughts, forget it. I don't need your answers, which probably wouldn't be truthful anyway.' He extended a hand. 'Enjoy the rest of your stay.' And then, because he did remain curious nonetheless: 'How long you here?'

'Just a few days,' replied the other, grasping the question much as a drowning man might a lifejacket. 'It was all very last minute. Got an unexpected call from a travel agent I sometimes use, saying there was this amazing deal, summer time in the mountains, real cheap, and you know me: when did I look a gift horse in the mouth! Also had some leave due. So I dropped everything, flew out yesterday and here I am, moseying about. It's a beautiful spot. And if you're here too, hey, even better! I could do with some company. Meet up later for a drink? I'd really like that. Lots to catch up on.'

'No,' said Simon. 'I don't think so. *Ciao*, Richard!'

And without further ado, he turned away as Richard said softly: 'Alison wasn't just me. She also played her part.'

Not that this made Simon pause.

'I really don't need to know,' he reiterated over his shoulder. 'It makes no difference now. None of it does. You have at least shown me that much.'

Conditions underfoot made the going slow and there was ample opportunity for him to look back had he wanted to. But only as he reached the main building did he turn, by which time Richard's purple anorak with its yellow stripes was nowhere to be seen. He might even have been imaginary.

Inside again, Simon knew he should go in search of his travelling companions, who might otherwise start wondering whether he'd maybe slipped on the ice or something. Auntie M particularly and he reckoned he'd upset her enough for one day. That stupid outburst on the train – further proof, if any were needed, of how jumpy this return to the Alps was making him. But Richard's unanticipated appearance had stirred too many memories, memories that couldn't be ignored, and he had first to find a nearby bench in order to make some sense of them all. Appraise their true significance.

Unsurprisingly, Alison was at their core. Be it at Sunday school, Sunday lunch or on virtually any other day of the week, come to that. He was often with Alison, upstairs usually, in her bedroom; else she was with him in his, playing whatever games they liked to play at whatever age. Anything from planting imaginary flags on unknown lands to keeping shop to doctor and nurse, a later form of exploration. Or they might listen to music. Read. A lot of reading. Or just talk. They also loved to talk.

They were in the same class and it was as they'd come out of school together one day to find Alison's mother by the gate – normally they went home unattended – that he'd learned about the death of his parents. The hurtling lorry. The ambulance, which hadn't managed to get them to hospital in time. The fact that his aunt would be on the next plane home, would take care of everything, so he wasn't to worry. Jesus has His reasons, said Alison's mother, clasping him awkwardly to her bony body, and everyone would be praying for him. The whole congregation. He wasn't alone. With Jesus, no one was. Not ever.

Then he'd noticed Richard in the distance, watching intently. Richard who, ever since the skiing trip, had been acting differently. Who would soon start publicly teasing him for being such a sissy. And it was this fact, above any other, which caused the tears to flow. Richard's defection; that's what had hurt the most. Even if he was being a sissy to show it.

'Flash Richard!' Alison had said once, after Simon first admitted to having him as a friend. Best friend, what's more. 'Richard's best friend is Richard himself. He'll end up harming you. See if he doesn't!'

Excepting that she herself, only a year or so later, would choose to dance with flash Richard at a school function. Dance and then date! Unbelievable! Although because he and Alison were such firm friends, this didn't mean they therefore stopped seeing each other. Maybe things weren't quite as smooth, or as easy, as before, but there was never any actual break – and he now recalled a hot summer afternoon when he'd gone round to Alison's to return a book he'd borrowed. Because here was another thing: seeing Richard hadn't stopped Alison from pressing books on him.

Alison's angular mother opened the door. She also had a book in her hand. In her case, the Bible. What else?

'Hello, Simon,' she said. 'Alison's in her room. I've baked a cake, you can tell her. For later. You're most welcome to stay.'

Alison's room was at the top of the stairs. You could walk straight into it and so, because the door was ajar, this is what he now did, only to discover that Richard was lying on the bed alongside her, the two of them umbilically linked. They were listening to music on Richard's mobile, one earphone apiece, and it was the looping white wire of the earphones that connected them. Though Richard did also have a bronzed hand on her stomach and, owing to the heat, was in a rucked T-shirt that exposed much of his own stomach, plus the neat line of dark hair that ran from his belly button into his shorts, which were of some clingy material that in turn revealed far too much of what he and Alison might have been up to while listening to their music. It was all Simon could do to keep his eyes on Alison's face as, blushing fiercely, he mumbled his thanks for the book and deposited it on her desk. Then immediately left.

For a short period after this, Simon avoided Alison completely and they did stop seeing each other. There was most definitely a break. But within weeks, she'd hunted him down and, having burst into tears, was apologising profusely for, as she put it, 'being such a shit. Stabbing you in the back like that'.

'I don't know what I was thinking,' she said. 'No, that's wrong, I do. I wanted to outrage the parents. Rattle my cage. That's what it was really all about. Finding the best way of pissing them off. But to do it with Richard! When I know how he treated you. I'm glad we're breaking up. Though do you want to know something, Si? He used to talk about you all the time. Like he was obsessed.'

And now, in the light of what had passed between himself and Richard on the glacier, he saw something that at the time he'd only been dimly aware of, if at all. As he'd walked into Alison's room that hot summer afternoon, far from trying to hide what was happening in his shorts, Richard had in reality been flaunting his condition. It hadn't just been Simon. There was need in Richard's eyes too. Need mixed with fear. Both maybe greater than his own.

'Ah, there you are! My, but you look a million miles away. And a little peaky, if you don't mind me saying. Are you all right, Simon, dear?'

Auntie M returned him to the present with a thud, as only Auntie M could.

'Sorry,' he said, scrambling to his feet. 'Just lost in thought.'

'You didn't let yourself get too cold, did you?'

'No, just thinking a few things through.'

'Because you do look uncommonly pale! What things?'

'Alison, if you must know.'

Margaret frowned. 'Ah!' she said. 'Yes, I wish she could have come too.' She shrugged. 'But she didn't and there's an end to it. No use crying over spilt milk. Talking of which, we've just had a rather nice cup of coffee. And some excellent strudel. Haven't we, Geoffrey? Maybe you'd like some too? Before we go any further. Pep you up a bit. Or should we find Cody first, do you think? Where can the elusive creature have got to?'

***

Cody was in fact assessing Lindt Heaven, officially opened some years before, as he'd just learned, by Roger Federer. On a large screen above one of the shop's counters a chocolatier was explaining in detailed close up how the chocolate was made. Although not grippingly enough to snare the shoppers' attention. The finished chocolates were what interested them more – despite the exorbitant prices.

Cody made a mental note not to bother shepherding his charges in this direction. He didn't imagine they'd be particularly enthralled by the chocolate process either, and they certainly wouldn't welcome the cost. Or was he thinking more of himself for a change? Since none of this set his own pulse racing exactly. But then, he thought somewhat mournfully, as he turned away, what did set it racing these days, travelling-wise? His gap year, when every new city, every new country, had brought him to fever pitch felt all too distant.

Oh dear! This morning's eruption of self pity, when (a tad theatrically perhaps) he'd seen himself as being continually confined to some poky back room, with a limited view of just a car park, was obviously not yet over. He must get a grip! It wasn't helpful to be thinking along such lines, especially at the start of a new week with a complicated job to bring off; a job moreover that he did ultimately value; that had its challenges, sure, but what job worth the doing didn't? And he had quite enjoyed walking through Wengen with Simon in the early morning. No, it wasn't all bad. Not by a long chalk.

He was on the stairs, going down, where he now happened to pass, coming up them, the player called Richard, whom he'd been tracking earlier to make sure that he and Simon connected successfully. From the latter's demeanour, it was blatantly clear, even in passing, that whatever had transpired on the glacier hadn't much dented Richard's sense of self-worth. There was maybe a hint of ruefulness about the guy; but only a hint; in the end, his cockiness was more apparent and, as a result, Cody felt an irresistible urge to bring him down a peg or two. For Simon's sake, he told himself. Who else?

He'd taken every precaution to stay out of sight where Richard was concerned and so it was an easy matter for him to make two things happen in quick succession. Looking over his shoulder, he saw that a pretty young woman in a lime green jumpsuit was also descending the stairs and he therefore caused her to drop her bag, which then had Richard bending to pick it up for her.

There was a short exchange.

'I'm so sorry.'

'No problem. My pleasure.'

'I don't know what happened.'

'I get the chance to talk to you.'

Which of course only made her hurry on downwards. Richard then swung round to look after her and that's when Cody put himself in Richard's line of sight, just as the woman went past him. Meaning that Cody now became the focus of

Richard's attention. Cody who knew exactly, but exactly how to harness his looks if so required.

It was a complex moment. Cody stood stock still, returning Richard's gaze with a frankness that the other couldn't possibly ignore; and he saw the same degree of hunger and greed in Richard's eyes, the same uncertainty, the same fear, the same dash of self-loathing and revulsion, as someone else once had.

That should take care of your cockiness for a little while! he thought contentedly, before turning tail and continuing on his way with as much insouciance as he could muster.

'We were beginning to think,' said a relieved-sounding Margaret, coming towards him with both Simon and Geoffrey in tow, 'that we might have lost you. Or you us! We've had our coffee and now we're ready for the ice palace. Assuming that's still on the agenda?'

'It most definitely is, if that's what you'd each like. Because may I please remind you – I did say, remember – that you're the ones in the driving seat. It's your show, this. You don't ever need to wait on me or ask my permission. But anyway – shall we?'

The ice palace turned out to be more dungeon than palace, running as it did right under the glacier in a series of interconnected tunnels. All the same, it was impressive. You entered down a steep steel staircase and at once the gleaming ice was all around you. The floor (also ice) looked highly polished and there was a handrail in case you slipped. At points, the curving walls had a blue-green tinge and there were a bewildering number of alcoves containing ice sculptures: bears, penguins, an igloo. Even, bizarrely, Charlie Chaplin in his role as the tramp.

'Would you like a group picture?' asked Cody as they emerged from a smaller, narrower side tunnel, less well-lit than the main ones, where they'd had to walk in single file. 'Over here perhaps? Next to the sculpture.'

They stood against the handrail and, after he'd taken the photo with his phone, Cody said: 'I'll email you each a copy.'

This was the first of his photos and, as such, it perfectly encapsulated the initial stage of their trip. Or that's what Geoffrey would later think anyhow. Margaret stood in the middle, with Geoffrey to her left, Simon to her right. Simon had his hands dug deep in his pockets and seemed to be scowling. You couldn't be wholly sure; the cap he was wearing, which he hadn't thought to take off after coming inside, shaded too much of his face. Margaret's hands were folded together, almost in prayer, and her head was tilted slightly to one side; Simon's side. She appeared a bit flustered, as if she maybe found the palace too maze-like, too complicated. Whereas Geoffrey, despite the chill coming off the ice and just a pullover with which to counter it, had struck a pose of some confidence. Head held high, feet planted firmly apart, arms akimbo, it looked like he was aping some intrepid arctic explorer. Would he reach the pole, did one think, or would he perish in the attempt?

And in the background: the imprecise, ice-sparkly shape of what might have been a large stalking bear.

Cody pocketed his phone. 'And that's about it for now, I guess,' he said. 'Up here at any rate. In terms of things to do and see. We should maybe think about heading back.'

They didn't talk much on their way down, each appearing lost in thought. All part of a necessary decompression, you might say, after being at the Top of Europe. Until, on reaching the hotel, where they found the hallway to be empty of suitcases, the Chinese contingent having gone on by now to their next destination, Cody broke their mutual silence by suggesting: 'How about, after a shower or whatever else anyone needs to do, we congregate on the terrace for a drink? We'll also be eating out there, I think. The food looks to be pretty good. I did check the menu.'

And indeed, the food was exemplary; they could all agree on that by the end of the evening. That and the undoubted congeniality of their surroundings. For as the light slowly leached from the scene, the snow-capped mountains, having passed from white through a sunset pink to a soft shade of grey, slowly merged with the sky to form a uniform blanket of darkness that enfolded the entire valley. The cowbells stopped their music, lights twinkled and Margaret found she didn't even need her cardigan, the air was still so warm.

'Awesome!' exclaimed Geoffrey, borrowing a word he'd heard Simon use more than once. 'Today's been just awesome. Hey, Simon? Only question: can tomorrow trump it?'

Day 3

The sound of a cuckoo's call, closely followed by a chime, was what roused Simon the next morning, letting him know immediately that they must still be in Switzerland. He wasn't sure quite how many bird-calls and chimes there'd been, but as they hadn't set a specific time for breakfast, did it even matter? He reckoned he could remain a while longer in the comfort of his bed. And boy was it comfortable! The pillows larger than he was used to, and wonderfully soft; the duvet luxuriously warm; the mattress perfectly calibrated as to how it did and didn't yield to the weight of his body.

Which is not to say that all this Swiss precision in the slumber department had been of any help when it came to sleep itself. It had been a troubled night, teeming with too many dreams, images, memories. The usual empty and forbidding square of course, but also Richard, Alison, his parents, Auntie M. The whole of his existence, unleashed it would seem by that encounter on the glacier, then tied in a tortuous knot which he knew he must disentangle were he to stand any chance of moving forward in a coherent manner.

He tried to order what, in his dreams, had been an out and out jumble, starting with his first sharp memory of Alison at Sunday school.

Church happened every week – his parents would have died rather than miss a service; or should it be that they feared they would die, and die irrevocably, if they did miss one, in that they'd thereby be precluding eternity for themselves? – which, for him and the other younger children, meant Sunday school in a side room, where they were told simplified Bible stories they could then draw. There were tables to sit at for the drawing and he and Alison were always put at the same one, presumably because their parents were such close friends. He couldn't remember ever choosing Alison *per se*. She was simply there, at his side, colouring Jesus's hair bright pink.

'Alison!' Ursula, the woman in charge, was outraged. 'What are you doing? And look! Have you ever actually seen a sheep that's all green? Honestly! Black maybe. But I like your wise men. They should be colourful.'

In Alison's world, however, things were seldom as they should be. Alison didn't like should. And although, at that juncture, she did redo the drawing, leaving the white of the paper exposed for the sheep, then some bright yellow for Jesus's curls, on future occasions she would continue to draw not quite as required. While also encouraging Simon to do the same – if he dared. Which normally he didn't.

Then, after church, their two families would lunch together at one or other of their homes and when Alison and he had been allowed down from the table, they would run into the garden or go to their rooms to play unsupervised. And here, since there was no Ursula watching over them, Simon did let himself be led by Alison. She it was who found for them the books they weren't supposed to read. Used forbidden words. She it was who eventually insisted they play nurses and doctors. Who first kissed him and felt him there, where she shouldn't.

And she it was who made him take his first tentative steps towards questioning the faith of his parents. Quite how Susan and Henry had come to be born again had never been clear to Simon. Their own parents hadn't been particularly religious, not as far as he'd been told anyway. Tepid C of E at most. Yet Simon's were passionately and unremittingly born again and life at 44 (the number of their house) revolved around daily Bible readings, friendships with other members of the congregation, countless drives to raise money for the church, choir practice and the weekly culmination of all this ardent theism: the Sunday service, long and full of revivalist praise. With added sustenance of a more material nature in the church hall afterwards: cakes, sandwiches and urns of over-brewed tea.

To begin with, Simon hadn't minded. Hadn't really given it much thought, to be honest. It was simply how things were and the fact that other children in the village didn't usually share his background was of little import because he and his family seldom mixed with those outside the church.

Then Alison had given him a present.

She knew Simon loved the Narnia Chronicles, so for his twelfth birthday had bought him *Northern Lights*, the first of Philip Pullman's *His Dark Materials* trilogy. Quite unwittingly, it must be said; she didn't realise at the outset that where the one was underpinned by Christianity, the other was most assuredly not. Although when this did become evident – being the point at which Alison finally read the books for herself, after Simon had finished with them, since by now he owned all three – a whole new light was shone upon their world.

'She's so amazing!' Alison had enthused of the trilogy's heroine, Lyra, as they sat one day on her bed, the books between them; they'd been comparing favourite bits. 'Nothing seems to frighten her. If something needs doing, she goes out and does it. Just like that. She can really, I mean really, think for herself.'

Being male, Simon had related more to Lyra's friend, Will. But he could see what Alison meant. Lyra was exceptional.

'And you do realise,' continued Alison excitedly, 'that the writer is actually an atheist? He hates the church.'

'No, who told you that?' For Simon had sensed none of this during his own reading of the trilogy.

'Miss Evans. He doesn't believe in Jesus in the least, not in the least, she says. Or God. Not even the tiniest little bit. And he's really, really critical of the church too.'

'Miss Evans says all of this?'

Alison nodded. 'When she heard what I was reading, she told me I must find out more.' Miss Evans was their PE teacher and, of all the staff, Alison's number one. 'You should do the same,' she concluded. 'Why don't you?'

Here they were interrupted by a shout up the stairs from Alison's mother. 'Tea time! There's cake if you want. And Alison, bring down your laundry when you come. I'm doing another load.'

Thus had begun a crucial life journey for him, although it would be a long while yet – years, in fact – before Simon reached the point where he now stood, free of religion altogether. And in the meantime, there were related matters to deal with on the way to adulthood. Like Richard, who could claim Simon's attention even while Alison's mother was breaking the news to him of his parents' death. Although this was perhaps also because he'd never been that close to his parents. They who'd never allowed for closeness. Since God had been their focus. The Bible. Jesus, but without the pink hair. While he, even before he'd begun to question things, was hardly ideal family material himself, given the feelings that Richard could inspire in him. Was he truly the sort of son they wanted?

There came a whirring sound and the cuckoo in the clock gave a single, piping call. Quarter past the hour, he guessed, although with the curtains drawn he couldn't be sure which hour exactly. Besides, he wasn't quite done with his memories. Or they with him.

Because now he must of course add Auntie M to the mix. His only relative of any significance, even though she'd gone away, to distant Argentina, when he was still in nappies. (He didn't count his grandparents, one set of whom – those on his mother's side – were either dead or spoken of as such, he wasn't a hundred per cent sure what the real story was; while the other [his father's parents] had long since vanished to New Zealand, where they'd gone to be near his father's estranged brother, an uncle whose name he didn't even know.) These grandparents, the New Zealand ones, would dutifully send him cards on his birthday and at Christmas, sometimes with small amounts of money enclosed; but never anything in the way of news. Unlike Auntie M, who'd sent tons of cards *and* parcels *and* letters, quite long letters, telling him all about her life in Buenos Aires. So that when, within a day or so of the crash, she appeared on Alison's front step, she looked quite familiar from the photographs she would include in her letters and parcels, but with an unusual smell about her, something quite spicy, which totally enveloped him as he stepped into her arms, letting her hold him tight.

'I'm here now,' she'd whispered in his ear. 'You don't have to worry anymore, Simon, darling. I'm here now.'

Whereupon she'd taken him home so he could sleep in his own bed again. Although in those early days, they'd often gone round to Alison's to eat – 'Until I work out just what an English boy likes to see on his plate!' Margaret had said with a sighing laugh. She'd also pronounced: 'A new start. That's what we both need. A brand new start.' Moving them in consequence to a brand new house on the other side of the village.

Not unnaturally, it had taken Simon time to adapt. There was, after all, a great deal to get his head around. Especially as, by now, Richard was openly and cruelly teasing him in front of the whole class for being such a sissy, as Richard liked to put it. Had Simon been left alone, he might just about have been okay. Yes, he missed his mother's cooking – Auntie M's was good, but undoubtedly different, another thing to get used to – and he still dreamed sometimes that he was throwing a ball in the garden with his father, who'd smile and clap as in church if Simon managed to catch what was chucked at him. But this wasn't what made him cry himself to sleep most nights. For that, you had once again to finger Richard.

However, with time, things did gradually improve. He'd always liked Auntie M's chatty letters, with their all-consuming interest in what he was doing and thinking, attentiveness also to the world about her – she'd a vivid way of describing life in exotic Buenos Aires, so removed from Suffolk. And now, in the flesh, the spicy flesh, as she set about creating a new home for them both, never giving the slightest sense of missing South America, he quickly came to feel even closer to her. Aunts, he decided, were a good thing. Most definitely. Every boy should have one. And when he learned that Auntie M and his mother had never seen eye to eye – although she wouldn't go into detail; not fair, she said, with Susan no longer around to put *her* side of the story – this rather validated his own misgivings about his parents and he felt even better. New starts: devoutly to be wished.

Though devout was maybe not the best word, since at around the same time he and Alison were having the Pullman conversation and he now recalled an afternoon when Alison had unexpectedly appeared at the house, eyes red from crying. He and Auntie M were in the garden, adding compost to a bed in the corner that she was wanting to revitalise, when Alison came stamping across the grass towards them, a crumpled tissue in one hand.

'Alison, dear! Is everything all right?' asked Auntie M, looking up concernedly.

'Do you mind if I hang out here for a while?'

'Of course not!'

'It's just that I can't bear to be at home right now. Not with them I can't.'

'This calls for a pot of tea,' said Auntie M. 'Or would you prefer lemonade? I think we've still some in the fridge. Then you can tell us what's happened. Come on, Simon! Put your trowel down, don't just stand there!'

Over tea and lemonade and some inevitable cake – because following the shaming example set by Alison's mother, Auntie M had also become an habitual baker – Alison told them how, as a result of letting her parents know about liking Philip Pullman, they'd bought her a book on the man's writing as a whole. A book that purported to be a balanced assessment, except that it wasn't. No way, said Alison. Too propagandistic for that. Too religiously inclined. Fanatical even in its denunciation of Pullman's atheism.

'They're so blinkered! Only ever see one side of things. Their side. So I've told them that I just can't be like that any more. Their way isn't my way, it never will be, so now they're mightily pissed off. Sorry, Margaret!' (From the start, Auntie M had insisted on first name terms.) 'Don't mean to swear.'

'Well,' said Simon's progressive aunt. 'As it happens, I've never been one myself for too much certainty. I do of course have my faith, as you both know, but I've always thought it a very personal thing, faith, and I'd never presume to tell anyone else what they ought or ought not to believe. We have to search these things out for ourselves. And don't let anyone ever convince you otherwise.'

Which was very much Auntie M's way, Simon was coming to realise. Another example being what had happened after the accident and the service for his parents in their church, after the crematorium and the ensuing expectation on the part of the congregation, Alison's parents prime among them, that Simon would continue attending services. Why wouldn't he, after so many years? But when he'd asked Auntie M if she minded whether he didn't for a while (he couldn't have said precisely why at that stage; it just felt a bit much), she'd not placed a single obstacle in his path. Nor had she suggested, other than mildly, just in passing, that he accompany her to the Catholic church. She seemed quite content for him to do as he pleased for the time being and when, as did happen once, a few members of his parents' church came round to ask when he was coming back, she told them in no uncertain terms to mind their own business. Couldn't they let the poor boy grieve in peace? Call themselves Christian!

And she said as resolutely to Alison in the garden: 'You'll always be welcome in this house, dear, you mustn't hesitate to come over just as often you want. We'll always be here for you. Won't we, Simon? I know what good friends you two are. So lovely.'

Though it wasn't long after this that Alison began going with Richard, upending Simon's world all over again. Added to which, Auntie M, usually so perceptive, didn't appear to understand, not even remotely, what was occurring. She thought Simon was distraught only because he wanted to become Alison's boyfriend himself! Not that she voiced this notion, mind, not then at least, but all the same – it was quite apparent to Simon that he couldn't possibly tell her the true state of affairs. Her concern for him was prey, he realised, to as many false expectations as any other adult's. Her Catholicism might be gentler than Susan and Henry's strident Evangelism, but it still didn't, still couldn't countenance certain behaviours. It too jumped to all the wrong conclusions. And so, like his parents before her, Auntie M became someone else who needed keeping at arm's length when it came to the matter of Richard and all that his feelings for Richard could and did imply.

What's more, after Alison had dropped Richard like the hot potato that he was and they were back to being proper friends again, then Auntie M did give full voice to what previously she had only thought. She'd come out with things like:

'I never did care for that boy. Alison's well rid of him.'

Or: 'I do hope you'll ask Alison to supper on Saturday? I'm trying a new recipe, tell her.'

Or: 'Do you and Alison maybe fancy a cinema outing on Friday?'

Or: 'It does me a power of good, seeing the pair of you together, how much you enjoy each other's company. So, so lovely.'

There was something else as well, not as crucial maybe, but telling nonetheless: her conviction that he was wasting himself at the garden centre working for Malcolm. Should rather be at university, like Alison now was, studying something 'worthwhile'.

'You've a good mind,' she would say. 'You should follow Alison's example and put it to proper use.'

When in point of fact it was the plants more than anything else that kept him sane. Ever since, with Auntie M, he'd started helping her in the garden as a boy, he'd felt their subtle power. Been under their spell. Loving the way that time would magically alter and become extended when he was concentrating on them. 'Gardening time', he liked to call it. Dreamy and different to the other sort, of which he was now reminded by a very insistent little wooden cuckoo.

Throwing back the duvet, he swung out of bed and went to draw open the plum-coloured curtains. Resolving, as light flooded the room, that today, if he did nothing else, he would at last tell Auntie M the whole truth – and nothing but the truth! – about himself by making continued use of awesome Alison. The Alison who'd coloured Jesus's hair pink. Who'd told him never to trust Richard. Who'd admittedly then gone on to date Richard, but who'd eventually apologised and who was now as close to him as ever. And who'd recently returned from uni on vacation in a new guise. A new look for a new persona, which of itself could, he now realised, help him to deal with his own difficulties. Why had he not seen this before?

Alison was currently in the third year of a law degree and, on each successive return home, there'd been something different about her. Clothes, make-up, choice of music and books – changes that showed how she was growing ever more securely into herself. And now the haircut! Alison's hair, reddish in colour and slightly curly, had always been a prize attribute. Hours would be spent combing it as they talked in her room and she'd many ways of wearing it: loose; tied back; swept up; fussily ribboned when she was younger. But in her most recent incarnation, she'd cut it almost all off, making her look extremely boyish – she'd a colt-like frame in any case – and that was just the start.

'There's something I need to tell you,' she'd said.

To which he'd smiled: 'What? Thinking of dyeing it too? Jesus pink perhaps?'

'Well, pink *would* be appropriate.'

'I'm all agog.'

'But I don't want this going any further. Not in the village. Not yet anyway. Okay?'

'You mean your mum and dad?'

'They'll cut off my allowance or something, like they did with my pocket money after I told them I didn't believe in Jesus any more. Maybe worse. With them, who the fuck knows!'

Then she explained how she'd recently fallen in love with another of the legal students, one of her house-mates, a woman called Helen.

'Does that shock you, Si?'

'Of course not.'

'But you are a little surprised?'

'A little, I guess. There was Richard once, remember.'

She snorted. 'That was an aberration.'

'And you did like to talk about boys.'

'Maybe more for your sake.'

'My sake?' Though that was as close as they came to referencing his own sexuality.

'Listen!' she said. 'I know it's feeble of me and I don't like being feeble, but just at the moment I really don't want to rock the boat. They can be so extreme, my parents, so spiteful and it's all too recent. Helen and I are still getting to know each other. It might still go pear-shaped. But if you want to tell Margaret, that I wouldn't mind. I trust Margaret. She can keep a secret.'

So if he now took Alison up on her offer and told Auntie M the news, he'd be able to dispel any and all misapprehension regarding himself and Alison – point one – while at the same time explaining about his own muddled sexuality. Point two and task complete!

He looked towards the towering mountains in the distance, site of yesterday's encounter on the glacier. But would Auntie M be sufficiently sympathetic? That he would only know once he'd screwed up his courage and begun his confession.

***

Margaret had woken early and, having made herself a cup of tea in her room for starters, was now on the terrace, where she could more thoroughly enjoy the stupendous view. The day looked like it was going to turn out fine again. Yes, there were some puffs of cloud in the sky, putting her in mind of Cody's weather warning of yesterday; but otherwise the indications were that the temperature would unquestionably soar once the sun had cleared the mountains. Hot going then for the walkers she could see on the road below, setting off on their day's hike up the steep path towards the summer meadows above and the continuing clank of cowbells. She guessed that today's Chinese quota must be about their business too, having breakfast perhaps in the room that had been set aside for them. Though if Bruno were right, the poor souls would have only the one day in which to enjoy all this splendour, while she and the others were being granted a second. She wondered how the itinerary was arrived at? Apart obviously from what they'd told Cody were their favourite places. Before the week was out, they'd no doubt find themselves in Rome. Also Paris. But in what order? And for how long in each case? Then Amsterdam again maybe, to finish off? Was that how things would go?

Just as well, she thought, that despite a fairly questioning mind, her Catholicism resigned her to mystery. Faith! In this life, you needed faith. To be able to take certain key factors on trust. So, for the moment anyway, she decided simply to go with Cody's instructed flow. See where the day might lead without asking too many questions. Besides, the Alps were for Simon and if, as a result, he could somehow come to terms with himself, who was she to interrogate anything?

She heard light footsteps, then an equally light kiss was being planted on her cheek and he was asking in that well-modulated voice of his: 'Morning, Auntie M. Sleep well?'

'I did actually. Like your proverbial top. The mountain air, no doubt. Isn't that what they always say?'

'I guess.'

She caught a subtle note of something else in his voice besides modulation; a note of some uncertainty; some urgency too.

'What?' she queried, looking up at him.

He coughed, as if something had lodged in his throat.

'What?' she repeated.

'There's something I need to tell you,' he said, the note of urgency taking precedence. But then he paused and the uncertainty gained ascendancy.

'I'm listening,' she said encouragingly. 'But do please sit down, dear. It's making me nervous. You hovering like that.'

Before he could say another word, though, they were interrupted by a cheery 'Good morning!' and Geoffrey had joined them.

'Later,' whispered Simon, pulling out a chair for himself. 'When we're alone.'

Was it her imagination, or did he look a trifle relieved to have been saved from saying more for the time being?

'Of course,' she said. 'Whenever.'

'Another magnificent morning!' declared Geoffrey, also sitting himself down. 'I don't mind one little bit that we're still here. Do either of you? Lots more to see in these parts. Where's our man with a plan?'

In the event, however, Cody wasn't to join them until after they'd finished their breakfast, which is what they now turned to. Bruno got in first and, because there weren't all that many guests to attend to this morning – other staff probably handled the back room; or, more likely, its occupants had left already for their day's excursion – he'd time enough, while standing by their table, to tell them some family history.

It was Geoffrey who started him off. 'You said yesterday,' was how he did it, 'that the hotel had been in your family for three generations, I think you said. So how did your grandfather begin? I mean, it must be quite a thing to get going, a hotel this size!'

Bruno raised an eyebrow. 'You want that I tell you my family's story?'

'If you can bear it,' said Geoffrey. 'Who doesn't like a good family saga!'

Thus primed, Bruno began his tale with a man called Hans, who'd grown up near Frankfurt, where both his parents (Bruno's great-grandparents, that is) worked in a hotel owned and run by a local Jewish couple; he as night porter, she as overseer of the hotel laundry. The First World War had only just ended and the country was struggling. The hotel, however, was able to ride out the troubled times and Hans's childhood – he was born in 1925 – was pretty secure. He was an only child – a sister and a brother having both died in infancy – and, as such, was the treasured focus of his parents' hopes and ambitions. They wanted more for him, a good deal more, than to work as they did, so menially. But if Hans's father hadn't been a night porter, life for the family might have turned out very differently. Because it was thanks to the nature of his work that, in the mid-thirties, he was approached by a local official who asked whether, in addition to those who nightly came and went, he wouldn't mind also keeping an eye on his employers? Apparently the authorities suspected that the hotel might be a front of some sort.

Now Hans's father was a law-abiding man and, like many of his ilk, a nominal supporter of the Nazis, whom he saw as bringing much needed order to a beleaguered nation. But his loyalties also extended to his employers, who'd always been good to him – *and* to little Hans, whose education they were paying for privately. They had no children of their own, Bruno explained, and could see how desperately Hans's parents wanted for him to get on in the world. So, in the end, Hans's father decided not to become a spy for the authorities. Rather, he told his employers everything.

As a result, the Jewish couple left Germany to start a new life in Switzerland, where they had connections. Not only that, but once they'd sold the Frankfurt hotel, they opened a new one in the Alps. Bigger and better and still in need of Hans's parents, whom they'd persuaded to accompany them. Who else, they said, could keep their establishment as safe at night? The sheets as dazzling?

Mind you, commented Bruno, the parents might just as readily have said no. They were German through and through, had no personal argument with the powers that be. But they also wanted a secure future for their son and could see that the best way of ensuring this was by taking up their employers on their generous offer. Either that, or not only would they both be jobless, but Hans's education would suffer as well.

Hence, in the mid-thirties, Hans found himself living in Wengen, where he continued to be put through school. With the ultimate aim of attending university to study law. All funded by a couple he'd come to regard almost as a second set of parents, even though they were both well into their seventies by now.

Then war was declared and something wholly unexpected took place. Hans's mother and father announced their intention of returning home. They couldn't sit idly by, they said. Their place was in Germany, at the side of other Germans. But, and on this they were equally adamant, they didn't want Hans going with them. He mustn't interrupt his education. And luckily, the owners of the hotel were more than happy for the boy to remain behind. If he saw them as a second set of parents, they saw him as a surrogate son.

'War,' said Bruno. 'It does most strange things to people. I didn't know my great-grandparents and sometimes I struggle to understand what they did.' He shrugged elaborately. 'But they are not here and we cannot ask.'

They'd been killed, he went on to say, in a bombing raid within months of returning to Frankfurt, after which the Jewish couple had formally adopted Hans as their own. Which is how, after the war's end and before he'd even finished his studies, he came to inherit a hotel in Wengen. Imagine that!

The story had a rhythm to it that was all its own, strange and hypnotic. Much like a fairy tale. Which in a way it was, supposed Geoffrey, right down to the happy ending. For Hans at least.

'Again it is strange,' said Bruno. 'For the Jews under Hitler, what happened in former times, it was terrible. Europe can be terrible. But for my family, for the Grubers, in the end it was not so horrible. The only thing for sure: nobody runs away.'

Geoffrey said: 'What an incredible story! I was thinking: a kind of fairy tale. Or like a novel almost.'

No one (excepting maybe the ever alert Bruno) appeared to notice that Margaret, who was sitting stock still, as if in shock, had tears in her eyes.

'Someone should write it,' continued Geoffrey. 'Really.'

'Well, my grandmother,' said Bruno, 'after she married Hans, she did write everything on paper. I have her account still.' He frowned. 'But there is much that is not so necessary perhaps.'

'Meaning?' Geoffrey was intrigued.

'Oh...' He gave another shrug. 'People say a lot of things, cruel things, especially in later times and that's also why my grandmother put everything on the paper. People must not forget, she would say.'

'What sort of things?' Margaret broke her silence at last, having surreptitiously wiped away her tears with the back of her hand. A tissue would have been too obvious.

'People,' explained Bruno, 'said that Hans tricked the couple who were so kind to him. They said that the hotel must really belong to some other relatives. There were two cousins afterwards, they tried to challenge Hans in court. But he was legally adopted. Also, he knew the law himself of course. From his studies. The cousins, they did not win.'

'And in Germany beforehand?' queried Geoffrey. 'When Hans's father was asked to become a spy. Was there any truth in the hotel being a front, do you imagine?'

'But for what?' put in Simon. 'A front for what exactly?'

'So we think,' said Bruno, 'that maybe the couple who owned it were also helping other Jews leave the country. It's certain that by the time they arrived in Switzerland they were very wealthy and they left without any trouble themselves and that's something else people have asked about. How could all their money come from only one hotel?' He gave a final shrug. 'There is much that we shall never know. History keeps its secrets.' He took a step backwards. 'But now it is me who keeps you. Do you know what you want to do today? I am happy to give ideas.'

'That's very kind,' said Geoffrey, 'but we already have someone who's taking pretty good care of all that.'

'Then I will wish you a most happy day! And I will see you this evening.'

After Bruno had left, Simon said reflectively: 'I know I did history at school, where you do learn this sort of stuff, but it's only when you see or hear it for yourself that it really kicks in. Like with the Anne Frank house and that girl who was weeping her eyes out.' He shivered.

'Although sitting here,' said Margaret hopefully, having regained her composure, 'on a day like today, everything does seem...'

'In this small corner of the bigger picture,' said Geoffrey, 'perhaps. But elsewhere? Europe's history is, I fear, ongoing.'

'And what really bothers me,' said Simon, 'what makes me so bloody angry, is Brexit.'

'Brexit?' Margaret was caught off guard. 'Meaning what, dear, exactly?'

'Cutting ourselves off from everything,' said Simon. 'When what we need to be doing is remembering this history.'

'Hear, hear!' cried Geoffrey, nodding vigorously.

'I see,' said Margaret after a short pause. 'If we're to stand any chance of avoiding similar things in the future, you mean. We must learn from our mistakes.'

'It's all very short-sighted,' said Geoffrey.

'And shameful,' continued Simon, warming to his theme. 'During the referendum, why did no one think to argue, but really argue, the case for history? Because if you examine Europe's past, isn't that really why the union was formed? Apart from economics of course. To bring nations together. Make sure they don't start turning on each other again, as they used to. Instead of allowing outright lies to flourish about how much money we would save the NHS! It's pathetic. And as for immigration!'

'So, Geoffrey!' said Margaret brightly. 'Here's a thought. You said as much yourself: Bruno's story is like a novel. You could try writing it yourself.'

'And that would solve our little problem, would it?' countered Geoffrey.

'It's all right for the two of you,' Simon went on. 'You haven't still got your whole lives in front of you. Sorry, don't mean to sound harsh, but it's true, Auntie M! *You* don't have to live with the consequences in the same way that *my* generation will have to. And I haven't even got to global warming!'

'Indeed, indeed,' assented Geoffrey. 'I hear precisely where you're coming from, young man. It's shameful and it's stupid, all this Brexit nonsense, all this separatism, this pretending we're not all linked, and who knows where it will get us in the end! Everyone's in denial, but one thing's for certain: we Brits have shot ourselves in the foot. Both feet come to that. Most spectacularly.'

'All the same,' begged Margaret, 'please don't let us spoil what otherwise promises to be such a perfect day. A perfect day in a perfect place, whatever the history. Because there are also neutral spaces, remember. Like Switzerland. Some sanctuary here at least. Bruno's story also proves that, don't forget.'

'And here, in the nick of time, comes the man who can tell us just how we're going to spend the rest of this perfect day in this perfect place,' said Geoffrey with a palliative smile. 'Even has a map in hand.'

Cody was all in white still, as he'd been from the start, although this morning, unusually for him, he also looked slightly fussed. His blond hair could have done with more combing than it had apparently received and there was a fleck of shaving cream on his neck.

'Sorry!' he said on reaching their table. 'Had an unexpected call.'

'No need to apologise,' said Margaret. 'We've been...'

'Discussing Brexit, if you must know,' grinned Geoffrey. 'A quite brisk exchange of views too, as the newspapers would have it.'

Cody commandeered a chair. 'Yes, well,' he said.' I'm afraid it often comes up these days.' He laid his map on the table. 'In all of my groups. Can't be avoided really.'

Geoffrey reached for the map. 'But that's all over now,' he said. 'Hey, chaps? In the past already, while here in the present we're just dying to hear what might or might not be on offer for today. Assuming we've got the whole of it in this perfect place. Do we?'

***

Cody's unexpected call had been from Cedric.

'Morning! Not too early, I hope? I reckoned you'd be up.' The reedy voice was made even reedier by an unsound line, although this didn't for one moment lessen its power. Nothing could do that. 'How are things?'

'Not too bad.'

'Where might you be?'

'Wengen. Switzerland.'

'And afterwards?'

'Paris and Rome.'

'In that order?'

'All rather depends on how today goes.'

'Are they up?'

'The woman is, I'm fairly sure. Then she'll obviously be joined by the other two. We have breakfast out on the terrace here. The view's quite something.'

'I've never been, you know.'

'Neither had I, until yesterday. You should. It's very beautiful.'

The older man sighed. 'I was with a group in Verbier once. That I liked. Although I do remember how everyone always complained about the prices!'

'Well, Switzerland isn't cheap.'

'Nothing of value comes cheap.' Cedric laughed briefly. 'But I'm not here to indulge in – dare I say it? – cheap philosophy.'

'Ha, ha!' Cody did his mentor the courtesy of laughing with him. 'Very funny. So what is it then, if it isn't cheap philosophy?'

There was a pause, making Cody fear for the signal. Had it been lost perhaps? But then he heard Cedric say quite clearly: 'It's just that the last time we were together – in that funny little bar you took me to, remember? – I thought I detected a certain... restlessness, I suppose. Dissatisfaction almost. You didn't seem entirely yourself. That's all I'm saying. And I've been worrying.'

'Cedric, I'm fine.'

'You don't need to pretend with me. I understand better than anyone about the job, how it can wear one down. Being responsible for other people all the time; it's never easy. The rewards come at a price. Rather like Switzerland!' There was another reedy laugh, although this time Cody didn't join in. 'Anyhow, I've been mulling it over and what I'd like to suggest is a complete break for a while. After this week is out. Would you consider such a thing? Please! Taking some time for yourself. Yourself and only yourself. Would you?'

Uncanny! Cody was thinking. *I half admit something internally and up he pops to articulate it. More forensically than I ever could. He doesn't just know my own thoughts. He is my own thoughts.*

'Cody?'

'That's very kind of you,' Cody heard himself saying. 'Thank you. I'll...'

'Do it?'

'Think about it. Promise.' Although the shock of Cedric training a spotlight on such barely acknowledged thoughts and emotions was making it hard for him to keep his voice level.

'I do hope,' said Cedric tartly, 'that you'll not just think about it. Thinking is all very well, but it's not the same thing as action and I am in earnest.'

'I hear that.'

'Loud and clear, I trust. Despite the dodgy signal.'

And so, after some further, less unexpected discussion of the week ahead and its possible shape, the call had ended, leaving Cody to stare ruminatively and for the longest of whiles out over a car park to which he'd already paid too much attention; until at last a sense of duty regained the upper hand and he picked up the map he'd been consulting before bed, said a wry farewell to the SUVs and Sports Sedans and headed for the terrace with its altogether superior view.

In the lobby he encountered Bruno, silently and with supreme concentration counting a pile of suitcases. Although at Cody's approach, presumably not wanting to be distracted, the proprietor at once began counting out loud.

'Eighteen, nineteen, twenty...'

Taking the hint, Cody smiled in silent sympathy as he passed. Then, emerging onto the terrace, he was himself in the thick of it again. He saw Geoffrey look up from where the group was seated and say something to the others that caused all three of them to stare expectantly in his direction. Three sets of eyes, each requiring another rabbit from the hat.

In keeping with his allotted role, therefore, he soon had his map out and, while Geoffrey opened it, was pushing aside the remains of their breakfast so that the map, a large one, could be smoothed out across the whole table.

'This is where we are,' he began, 'this valley here, and this was yesterday.' He pointed to where the contour lines coalesced.

'Today I was thinking we can perhaps go down instead of up, take a boat ride on this lake over here maybe. Unless anyone has anything else they'd especially like to do?'

But no one had and, in consequence, the lake it therefore was and before too long they were on another train, chugging downhill through a selection of small stations, where more summer walkers and a variety of other less energetic-looking visitors got on and off in such numbers that empty seats soon became scarce. There was no equivalent problem, however, on the boat they boarded to take them across the lake; here they could spread out. Accordingly, Geoffrey took up position at the prow, Margaret stood nearer the stern, while Simon, who, Cody was pleased to note, definitely looked like he was readying himself for some task, lingered for a short while amidships on one of the benches there that had an awning over them, making it quite easy for Cody to engage the young man in a moment's private conversation.

'Pretty,' he said. 'Isn't it? Classic chocolate box territory.'

Simon nodded abstractedly.

'Though I guess I do also owe you an apology.'

'For what?'

'No snow.' Cody smiled. 'We haven't matched your memories in all respects, have we now?'

Simon turned to stare at the smiling man on the bench beside him.

'Tell me!' he said suddenly. 'How did you arrange for Richard yesterday? On the glacier, where of course there was snow. Tons of the bloody stuff.'

'You ran into someone you know up there?'

The two of them continued to stare at each other.

'But anyway,' said Simon eventually. 'However you managed it, I want to thank you.' Now he was the one to be smiling. 'It was very useful. Helped click certain vital things into place.'

'Funny,' said Cody, 'isn't it? How everything works sometimes. In a strange sort of unison. Like music. And if you still think, even with the smallest part of you, that Margaret doesn't want you exactly as you are, then... well, you're very much mistaken.'

Simon gazed across the sun-dazzled waters of the lake. 'She doesn't like it that I work in the garden centre though, that's for sure. And this morning she didn't much care for how worked up I got about Europe. Brexit and stuff. But then that was just my own nervousness, I guess. Knowing what I have to do today. And say.'

'In that case,' prompted Cody, 'you should go and do it. Without any further procrastination.'

Simon turned from the blue of the lake to look deep into two pools of sustaining green. 'The trouble is, I'm not very bold as a person,' he confessed. 'I needed the nudges. The guidance.'

'Oh, we all need help along the way,' replied Cody. 'To varying degrees. It's no crime, being human.'

'Except when it is a crime.'

'But what you're proposing isn't. Not for people with any sense.'

'So do you know where she is, by any chance? Auntie M.'

'Towards the stern,' said Cody. 'Last time I looked.'

He watched as Simon went in search of her, a young man on a mission, earnest-looking and intense, so much to deal with still. He saw too, in his mind's eye, himself at a similar age and was reminded of what Cedric had said during his recent call. *Thinking is all very well, but it's not the same thing as action.*

After a while, they came to a pleasant old town on the other side of the lake, where the boat docked for a couple of hours and they could all get off and wander round and have a spot of lunch. They crossed a bridge or two, admired some cobbled squares, in the second of which they settled at an outside café for sandwiches and beer. The sun was still shining. There were red geraniums in many of the window boxes and the woman who served them reminded Geoffrey of their waitress in Amsterdam. Consequently, when they ordered coffee to finish, he asked for the sugar in Romanian. She was a local, however; *zahăr* meant nothing to her. Only *zucker*.

Cody couldn't be certain – he didn't imagine there'd been enough time – but from the way in which Simon and Margaret were behaving towards each other, he sensed that the young man hadn't defaulted on his determination to explain himself. Or to at least start doing so. And when they re-boarded the boat after another leisurely stroll through the town, Margaret and Simon went immediately to sit apart again, near the stern once more, leaving Cody alone with Geoffrey, who was in philosophic mode.

'I've always been rather scornful of Switzerland,' the latter said. 'Pretty though it undeniably is. Orson Wells had it about right, I've always thought.'

'Don't you mean Harry Lime?'

'That film anyhow, where he says, give or take: *Five hundred years of peace and what the hell do you get? The cuckoo clock.* Nice to be neutral, but stuff happens most – and I should know! – when there's some element of struggle involved.'

Cody couldn't help but smile.

'What?' demanded Geoffrey.

Cody shrugged. 'Only that someone else was saying something pretty analogous this morning. Nothing of value comes cheap, was how he chose to put it.'

'Aha!' said Geoffrey. 'Your unexpected call.' He looked keenly at Cody. 'You do realise how much you intrigue us all? This whole damn set up. Who you really are. Where you come from. What training and for how long you've been doing it.

Who else is part of it. You can't have me believe the punters don't ever ask any leading questions!'

Cody met Geoffrey's interrogation without a flicker of demurral. 'So what would you like to know?'

But now Geoffrey found himself hesitating. It was the old conundrum. If he asked too much, did he risk spoiling the effect? Lessening the magic. Did he want to end up discovering that the wizard was in reality only a mild old man hiding behind a curtain? No! More prudent by far, he now decided, to follow another line of enquiry altogether.

'You probably already know this,' he said, with a quick, bitter bark of a laugh, 'but I was married to a woman called Isobel once and a few times now, over the past two days, I've had the oddest feeling that somehow, somewhere, she's on this journey with us. Just tagging along.'

'Uninvited?'

'Well, the old cow never did stand on ceremony! Might she be?'

'Is she so important to you?'

'She was. Now though? Now, I would rather hope not.' Then, seeing as no ready answer was forthcoming, he added with a toss of his head: 'But what was it that Margaret said this morning? Why spoil a perfect day? A perfect day in a perfect place. Even if it is Switzerland. Cuckoos and all. I have one in my room, you know. A clock, I mean.'

'I imagine everyone does,' said Cody. 'Goes with the mountain view.'

'Everyone have one of those too?'

'Not quite everyone.' He stood up. 'But talking of Margaret, I should really go and check on them.' He consulted his watch. 'Not long now till we're back where we started. Want to come?'

Geoffrey shook his head. 'I'll stay put, if you don't mind. Soaking up this wonderful view.' He threw wide his arms.

'Shouldn't be so down on it, should I? Eat your heart out Lindt Heaven!'

They weren't too far from the bank, along which were dotted some substantial villas, all with gardens that ran down to the water's edge. A few were shuttered; holiday homes in all likelihood. The majority, however, looked to be fully occupied and some even had people on their terraces, placed there as if by some meticulous director who wished to animate the scene. A woman in a wide-brimmed straw hat and some sort of summer robe, gaily patterned, lay on a lounger reading. She glanced up from her book and then waved. In close up, she was probably smiling too; but this detail Geoffrey couldn't hope to make out from the boat.

Meanwhile Cody, on his way to the stern, also had half an eye on the bank and, as another villa slid into view, this one shuttered, a sudden shiver caused his skin to tingle. To tingle and to burn. Had he given too much away, he wondered, back then? With Geoffrey. Because the uncomfortable truth was, Cedric's call had unsettled him greatly.

Restlessness, Cedric had said. Dissatisfaction. Not entirely himself. Or was this who he was fast becoming?

The larger lakeside villas were gradually reducing in scale to something more suburban. Soon they'd be back in the town they'd set sail from and must re-board the train and toil back up the hill to dinner on the terrace. The end of another perfect day! Friday tomorrow and then...? Soon he'd need to decide.

But first – first he must mould his little band into a moveable entity. Shepherd Margaret and Simon towards Geoffrey, who was much nearer the gangplank. Though as he continued sternwards, what he encountered there caused all logistical considerations to evaporate for a moment.

Margaret and Simon were the only people sitting on the benches at the back of the boat. They were sitting close, side by side, and Margaret had, in addition, an arm around Simon; was in fact hugging him tight, while with her free hand she was gently patting his shaved head, which lay pinkly on her shoulder. Had that meticulous director wanted to include them as models – or so Cody couldn't help thinking in that suspended instant – it would surely have been for a tender *pietá*. With a range of Swiss mountains as backdrop. Distant snow.

The tingle intensified.

Day 4

Echoing voices, and on the early side, were what woke Margaret the next morning; right outside her room too, which was very different in design and layout from the Swiss one. In Wengen, her wide bed had been just one piece of ornate furniture among many: the heavy wardrobe; a substantial chest of drawers; a fatly upholstered armchair; a bedside table with a thick marble top; an ornate brass lamp; all enclosed within walls of crimson. Here, by contrast, everything had been stripped away. The light filtering through the shutters of a small, square, unusually high window showed today's walls to be bare and whitewashed while, as to furniture, all that Margaret could see on opening her eyes was a simple wooden chair, a bedside table fashioned from bleached pine and, for a wardrobe, an alcove in one corner, partially obscured by a thin curtain. The tiled floor was without benefit of carpet. All quite, quite different.

She sat up, put her feet to the cool tiles and padded to the door. The voices were receding, but she could still make out a few words. *Mi scusi. Prego. Mille grazie.* No prizes then for guessing where they were! She opened the door a fraction. The corridor was long, also whitewashed and, at the far end of it, elongated shadows were being thrown against a segment of wall, the owners of the voices having vanished around the corner. She was obviously in something like a converted monastery. Or an old prison even?

Returning to the warmth of her simple, single bed, so unlike the one in Wengen, she found – unsurprisingly – that her waking thoughts were nevertheless taking her right back to Switzerland. And, more particularly, to Simon's unexpected confession of yesterday. With eyes fixed on the bare wall opposite, she re-lived the quiet, almost tentative way in which he'd come to sit with her near the stern of the boat. How, out of the blue, he'd started to talk about Susan and Henry. How strict they'd always been as parents. How distant and forbidding. Seldom warm.

Then came his memories of being at Sunday school with Alison. Plus certain other childhood recollections, like the skiing trip she'd underwritten, and that friend of his called Richard, whom she'd never much liked. Cocky little sod that he was!

There'd been a hiatus at this point while they stopped for lunch and a stroll through that pretty lakeside town, with her feeling fairly certain she knew exactly where all this was headed. How much Simon treasured Alison – that's what, in essence, he was wanting to tell her. Surely? And of course he'd have her blessing. After all, how often had she dreamed the same thing?

But once they'd re-boarded the boat and were back on a bench near the stern, a quite divergent story had emerged, coming as a total shock. More about Richard, but Richard as seen in a startling new light. A new slant too on the skiing trip. Even a meeting on the glacier yesterday. Imagine that! Then more about Alison, equally surprising. None of it at all what she'd been expecting – or hoping for, more to the point. Because in Margaret's vision of the future, Alison had figured far more centrally. Although Simon had ended his confession by saying that without Alison and Alison's example, he'd not have had the bravery to admit to his true feelings.

'I hope you're not too disappointed, Auntie M?' he'd asked in conclusion. 'I know how much you always wanted something else for Alison and me.'

'I only ever wanted...'

'Because we'll always be friends. That doesn't change.'

'I only ever wanted,' she repeated, 'for you to be happy, Simon. That's all it ever was, dear. Don't for a minute think otherwise. Please!'

Then, to prove her point, she'd taken him into her arms and held him as tight as she knew how.

But oh! What about all the other things? Her own part in all of this! If Simon could tell her the truth, didn't she therefore owe it to him to do likewise? Although, in her case, the corresponding muddle was beyond measure, painful beyond measure too, impossibly hard to grapple with, and the light of a new day didn't make any of it any the less so.

Jumping up, she went into the bathroom, which, as she discovered, was right off her bedroom, behind a second door. The shower was a powerful one and she turned it on full. Then, having dried herself, she returned to her bedroom to dress. And here was something else about this discombobulating trip! When she drew back the curtain which partially obscured the alcove, she found that all her clothes were laid out on the concrete shelves just as if she'd done the arranging herself. It had been the same in Switzerland. Yet she'd no memory of unpacking anything. Not a single item!

Continue going with the flow, she supposed. Remember and cling to Cody's exhortation. Until, hopefully, she'd be shown a feasible way forward.

Dressed, she ventured into the long corridor she'd peered down earlier. At its end she came to a deserted lobby – no one stood behind the desk, nor was there any sign that anyone ever had; the lobby's emptiness was profound – beyond which, on the other side of a glass door, lay an equally deserted little square. Sallying forth, she paused for a moment on the hotel steps to look appreciatively about her at the ochre buildings that formed the little square, all with shutters of one colour or another at their serried windows. She registered the single tree growing in one corner; the scooters parked in another; a cluster of metal tables and chairs in a third, belonging to some café that hadn't yet opened its doors. She remembered Rome as being noisy. But here, in this small corner of it early on a Friday morning, silence reigned. As if the world were waiting for her to flick a switch. Then she heard a faint, familiar stutter: an approaching scooter.

It was being driven by a young man with olive skin and hair the colour of honey – he was without a helmet – and it swept diagonally across the square, firing a series of mechanical burps and farts as it went.

Which part of Rome were they in, she wondered? Obviously not the centre. Too quiet for that. Trastevere? In which case, she couldn't be far from where she'd stayed on that fateful art trip. Should she go exploring? She consulted her watch, reckoning that as it was still so early, the others weren't likely to appear for breakfast until much later. Assuming a hotel as sepulchral as theirs ran to breakfast? And if she did go exploring and did then manage to find where she'd once stayed, why, she might even be able to pop into that church she remembered visiting one afternoon, even though she'd not been a believer back then. Back then, Susan had been the only believer. But still, something had taken her into that church with its funny statue of the Virgin Mary dressed in a gown of ruched satin, blood red and sequined.

In those days, it would never have occurred to Margaret to ask for intercession. She'd only noticed the statue because it had been got up so gaudily. But now? Now, being more in need of help than ever before, she wouldn't hesitate. Would be on her knees in a trice.

Again she looked about the silent square, soaking up its peacefulness. It went without saying, of course, that she was pleased that Simon had been able to confide in her. She'd known all along that something was upsetting him, had hoped this trip would clear the air. She was even prepared, at a pinch, to accept that it might be okay if he stayed working for Malcolm at the garden centre. Maybe university wasn't essential. But none of this could begin to solve her own dilemma: how to answer Simon in suitable kind?

***

Although Cody, busy shaving, wasn't unhappy with the way in which the Swiss section of the trip had panned out – rather the reverse; all in all, Simon had excelled himself – Cedric's unanticipated call had certainly thrown a spanner in the works. The persistence of that reedy voice and what that voice had so airily suggested: not easy to ignore.

Putting down his razor, Cody considered the foamy face that stared back at him from the bathroom mirror. There was nothing in the eyes, however, or his expression generally – outward appearances remained calm and steady; fit for purpose – to explain why, simply by articulating them, Cedric had allowed Cody's dissatisfaction and restlessness to erupt like they had from the box he'd so far, sort of, managed to contain them in.

Angrily, impatiently, he splashed away the last of the foam, towelled himself dry and strode back into his bedroom to dress in his customary work clothes, also fit for purpose. Trapped! The truth of the matter was, he felt imprisoned. By circumstance. By history. And, most of all, by his own dogged dependability. That outward calm. The unwavering steadiness. All an escalating sham.

He glanced about the room, so unlike the one in Wengen. More of a cell really than something four-star. Did this perhaps explain why he was thinking in terms of imprisonment? But no! The fault lay not in externals – Cedric's words; the inadvertent design of a hotel bedroom – but in himself, deep within himself. And if he wanted to uncover why he was feeling as he did, that was where he had to start looking: inwards.

He remembered something one of his friends from his early twenties, before he'd joined forces with Cedric and still had time for intimates, had said to him, after they'd been on a weekend away together.

'I don't know why,' the friend had remarked with a grudging smile, 'but when I'm with you, I never find myself worrying on your behalf. Whatever happens, I'm always sure you'll be all right. Lucky bastard that you are! What's the secret, mate? What's the trick?'

At the time, the remark had not displeased Cody. The flicker of protest he'd experienced – *Sometimes I need looking after too!* a part of him had wanted to cry – was fleeting. For who didn't wish to be unassailable? But now – now he was coming more and more to appreciate the negative side of capability. Of being perpetually 'all right'. It isolated you; made accessing your own feelings when setbacks did occur, as inevitably they must, increasingly difficult. Especially when your job demanded that you set your own needs aside anyway.

Cody sighed. For now another, even bleaker thought had struck. Choosing a life where the making of friends wasn't easy – wasn't one just begging to be isolated? And what if, in addition, appearing capable, calm and steady was actually a sneaky way of making sure you didn't ever have to access or confront your own feelings? What if he was running scared of his very self? Nothing more than a snivelling, pathetic, hopeless little coward!

Cedric was obviously spot on. He badly needed and must absolutely take a break. Step aside in order to peer long and hard at who and what he'd become. So! When the week was out, he reckoned he would, must grab the time and the space on offer. Project Cody! Starting right after this trip. No delays.

His phone was lying on his pillow. He began texting.

Hi Cedric! he tapped. *That break you talked about. Would it really be in order?*

He didn't have long to wait before his phone sounded a reply.

But of course, he read. *A last day in Amsterdam and then you can take off. Absolutely. I'm assuming you'll be following the usual pattern of ending the trip where it started? I would if I were you. But anyway, yes, of course, sure thing. Ring when you're back. How was yesterday?*

Great, he typed in relieved response. *The young man, Simon, was very brave. You would have been proud. Thanks, hey!*

Satisfied, he slipped his phone into the pocket of his jeans, remembering as he did so how tenderly Margaret and Simon had sat together on that bench on the boat. The pink of Simon's ears against the white of Margaret's blouse. The curve of his skull. A living *pietá* – and again his skin started to tingle.

***

Quitting the little square where the hotel was, Margaret soon discovered they weren't anywhere near Trastevere, but on the other side of the Tiber altogether, not far in fact from the city centre. No chance then of locating her old street quite yet, although she did pass a few promising churches and it was into one of these that she now slipped; a baroque affair with a vast nave, a multi-coloured marble floor and a high, arched ceiling covered in ornately painted panels whose subjects it was impossible to discern at a distance. All you knew for sure was that the images must be biblical. She noticed that a morning mass was on the cards, although as it didn't start for another half an hour and breakfast still loomed, she knew there'd not be time. Some solitary prayer was all she'd be able to squeeze in.

Predictably, she started with Simon, only coming to the others (Susan and Henry; the *Hogar de Caritas*; Gustavo) at the tail end of what she needed to ask *vis-à-vis* her principal focus. Then, because the marble floor was proving rather hard on her knees and she wasn't yet ready to forsake the building, she sat awhile as a flood of memories presented themselves to her in the form of an internal period movie. She saw her twenty-two-year-old self descend the narrow stairs of the *pensione* where they were billeted. She was wearing colourful slacks and a new top she'd bought in a street market the day before. A couple of the other girls from the art trip were behind her, giggling. The day was bright and an oblong of sunlight lay aslant the threshold of their building. In it stood a man with olive skin and hair the colour of honey, looking up at her and smiling. He stepped forward.

'I am Gustavo,' he announced, revealing a dazzle of teeth as his mouth made a pleasing shape around the accented words. He really was disgracefully good looking. 'I am come to take you to the Borghese Gallery. Best in all of Roma. I have tickets. There are ten, I am correct? But the others, where are they please? It is fourteen hundred hours already.'

Margaret was in the final year of a degree in Visual Arts and had been working weekends in a bar so as to afford this most longed for of trips. The painter who interested her most was Raphael and, in Rome, she knew there were some prize canvases. Also, of course, the Sistine Chapel. Many other paintings as excellent. St Peter's with its *pietá*. The Colosseum. Spanish Steps. The chance to throw a coin for good luck into the Trevi Fountain. Five days were never going to be enough.

But for Gustavo, all *he* needed was just the one and he made his move that very afternoon. She was standing before *La Fornarina*, Raphael's Portrait of a Young Woman, marvelling at the confident, knowing look in the subject's brown eyes. How had Raphael achieved this? And what did his technique say about his attitude towards women? She could just hear Mr Reynolds asking the question in class. Then all at once Gustavo was by her side, the look in *his* brown eyes every bit as mesmeric as anything Raphael had ever come up with.

'Sexy, yes?' Not the sort of question Mr Reynolds would have posed, but to the point certainly, given the woman's bare breasts and the position of that finger, just below the left one, making you imagine she might be about to squeeze or caress her own nipple. Not to mention the seductive drape of diaphanous material across her belly button, another point of ripe sensuality.

'He's my favourite too.' Though how did Gustavo know what she felt about Raphael? Merely from the way in which she was standing? 'If I could paint you, if you let me do that, I would paint like this also. Not so good of course, I am not Raphael. But sexy also. Even with clothes.'

'You paint?'

'That is why I do this job. Only reason. I have much time with the paintings. Every day I can come. It is an education. You want more tomorrow? I will bring you again.'

'I'm afraid we have the Sistine Chapel tomorrow. And I forget what else besides.'

'But this evening, this evening you don't do anything? You are free this evening, no? I come to the *pensione*. Okay? We go for a drink.'

'We do?'

'But of course! *Por supuesto!*'

That evening, therefore, after finding themselves a corner table in a nearby bar, where he told her all about himself – how he was studying to paint; that he was spending time away from his native city, Buenos Aires, because his course allowed for extracurricular study in a foreign one; that his father, Italian by birth, was a lawyer and didn't approve of art as a career, only his Argentinian mother was sympathetic to his wishes; that Buenos Aires was a great place to live, *muy estimulante* – so it came about that, after their third drink at their corner table, which was set slightly apart, he pulled her closer and began kissing her and those dazzling teeth of his were soon forming a new set of accented words as he implored her to come back to his apartment. It was very near, he whispered. Very nice. Better than a *pensione*. Big bed.

If asked, Margaret would have denied being a push over. High standards, that's what Margaret Thompson had. No go areas. Requirements. Which no other boyfriend had ever breached. But with Gustavo? He simply elbowed everything aside. Caution. Good sense. Inhibition. Everything.

The ensuing week was exhilarating in every respect. By day, she continued on the tour with the others, taking in galleries, buildings, piazzas, the lot. Until she felt thoroughly and gloriously satiated. Though not as satiated as by night. Late every afternoon he would be waiting for her outside the *pensione*, leaning lazily against a wall, would take her to 'their' bar for a drink, then back to his apartment. Basically a large single room with a very large bed in it, an easel, a stove and a sink. The toilet was on the landing. There he would paint her, fast and furious; the clock was ticking, after all; five days, that's all they had together. Then some pasta, some wine, before ending up on the large bed, where she would touch, trace, lick and marvel at every part of him. Until the portrait was finished – cubist in style; nothing of Raphael about it – and they must say goodbye because the next morning a bus was coming to take her to the airport.

'You will write?'

'I will write.'

'Will you miss me?'

'*Por supuesto*.'

'And so?'

'*Querida*, we will make a plan.'

'Promise?'

'Do you not trust me, *carina*?'

Back home, however, the promised letter never materialised, for all that she haunted the hallway every morning during those desolate, drawn-out days. Then the holidays were over and it was time to go back to uni and she had to ask Susan whether *she* wouldn't mind keeping a look out for post. Far from ideal, since she mistrusted Susan; always had, always would. Susan who'd forever been in a state of fierce and unfriendly competition with her older sister – over their father's attention, never easily obtained; the last helping of pudding; the best seat on the sofa; avoiding the washing-up. Anything and everything.

Margaret squirmed on the pew. Nifty, shifty Susan! She closed her eyes. Susan who seeped in everywhere.

In the days following Margaret's art trip, talk in the Thompson household might have – should have? – revolved around Rome and what, on the surface at least, Margaret had been lucky enough to experience there. It wasn't as if anyone else in the family had ever been abroad. Rome was special. Yet who now hogged the limelight? Susan, of course. Starting at dinner on the very day of Margaret's return, just as their mother was finishing serving, by announcing with a triumphant little laugh, all silvery, that she'd recently met a boy called Henry, a Christian as it happened, a proper Christian too, nothing half-baked about Henry. Also, she'd joined his church, she said, and was wondering whether they wouldn't like to come with her next Sunday? As guests.

'It's not at all boring,' she continued breathlessly. 'Not like sad old St Mary's. They sing a lot and there are guitars and they're all very friendly, they don't go around ignoring each other. They hug and they smile. You can actually feel the love, Jesus's love. It's electric.'

'Well, well!' exclaimed their mother. 'Although if you don't mind, my sweet, I'll stick to what I know.'

Mr Thompson said nothing. But then he seldom contributed to mealtime conversation.

'Will *you* come then?' Susan asked Margaret, throwing down another of her gauntlets.

'Can't on Sunday,' Margaret replied quickly. 'But I'm happy to meet Henry somewhere else if you want to arrange it.'

So Susan had done precisely that – coffee in Ipswich, in a newly opened place on the market square that played up-to-date music – and, rather to Margaret's surprise, Henry turned out to be not at all bad. Too earnest perhaps, and she couldn't entirely understand why he'd fallen out with his brother, which apparently he had. Something to do with his church maybe? But otherwise, he was quite sweet – and he clearly thought the world of Susan. He pulled out her chair with touching gallantry, passed her the sugar before helping himself, laughed immoderately at her jokes and never once interrupted while she was speaking.

'He's nice,' Margaret said on the bus home afterwards. 'Really nice.'

It was a rare instance of accord between the sisters and Susan cemented it by saying: 'I wish you could meet someone too. You're so pretty. Much prettier than I am. Isn't there someone at uni?'

For a brief moment, Margaret was tempted to confess about Gustavo. But something held her back and, by the time she asked Susan to watch the post, relations between the two of them had returned to their usual level of frostiness.

Wishing at this point to pause the period movie, Margaret stood up from the pew and turned towards the door of the church. But even as she made her pensive way back to the hotel, the film flickered on regardless.

She saw herself standing alongside Susan and Henry in their church on the Sunday she'd first agreed to accompany them there, surrounded by happy, clapping people.

She saw her mother at the sink, hands hidden in the foaming water and tears in her eyes as she explained to Margaret why their father had decided to leave home. 'He has needs apparently,' was how, between sobs, she'd put it, 'that I can no longer satisfy.'

She saw the letter her father had left for them, which mentioned only a need for freedom. 'I turn fifty next month,' he'd written. 'If I don't do this now, I never will.'

She saw herself in her bedroom, staring into the mirror on the girly dressing table she'd had since six and wondering, with a sinking feeling, why she'd let herself be seduced by a young man from Buenos Aires. Just because he was so good looking? So charming. Sexy. Had such a white, winning smile. Or did her own needs explain things better? In which case, what *were* her needs? Could she write them down with as much specificity as her father? Freedom! What was freedom anyway? When you thought about it.

She saw how her mother had lain in that hospice bed, pain writing a new sort of message across her stretched features. Fingers plucking at the sheet, as though she were playing a stringed instrument and you could coax music from bed linen. Then turning that stretched face to the wall.

She saw herself standing next to Susan in the crematorium, with Henry on the other side of her. Just the three of them. No father of course.

She saw Susan's hand reach out for her own. The way she'd gripped it. Herself in a shapeless dress. Henry looking smart, as he always did, in a blue blazer and a patterned tie. Dazzling white shirt.

She saw how the white flowers on their mother's coffin had started to wilt already. She saw the face of the priest from St Mary's, who'd come from the church service to the crematorium to be with them there too. Heard again his platitudes. She saw more of Henry. More of Susan. How the two of them had bracketed her. Hemmed her in. Or should that be supported her? Was that what she was seeing? Their undoubted care. Linked to her own soaring desire for freedom. A new start.

Whereupon she came once more into the peaceful little square where the hotel was situated to find that the café in the corner was open by now for business. There were chatting people at the metal tables, a seductive smell of coffee in the air and her period movie stopped unspooling.

***

To Geoffrey's pleased surprise, this oddest of odd trips was having a most beneficial effect on his journal and his daily jottings were mounting up nicely. As he remembered it, Hemingway had aimed for three hundred words per day. A modest but fine amount. ('Fine' being the apposite adjective when it came to Papa; he'd used the describer often.) Whereas Geoffrey was currently managing at least double that.

His pen was a handsome one – brass, with a steel-coloured nib – of a sort that Papa himself would not have been averse to wielding. The only pity being the feebleness of its actual owner. Well, that and its provenance: Isobel, of all people, on the occasion of their first anniversary. Now there was an irony! Especially when you were attempting to describe another sort of woman entirely, one whose company you were coming more and more to enjoy. At first, he'd not been too sure about Margaret. Her demeanour was so very strict. Off putting, you might even say. Yet he found that she was definitely growing on him. Strictness wasn't the whole story. There was empathy in there too. A hint of intriguing sadness. Quite apart from her physical charms.

Had his words done her justice? Looking them over, he decided that, on balance, they hadn't. Way to go still on the writing front, a phrase which she'd said put her in mind of war. As good an example as any of her perspicacity. He sighed, closed his journal, screwed the top back onto his Papa-like pen and went into the bathroom to attend to his ablutions.

The space set aside for breakfast, which he located down a long corridor connected to the lobby, was no less austere and prison-like than his own room had been. More bare walls were in evidence, and a high ceiling, another floor of uniform, rust-coloured tiles. But here food had been laid out on a sizeable sideboard with, mercifully, a quite un-prison-like generosity and, as Geoffrey inspected what was on offer, he was able to help himself – creature of habit that he was – to his usual orange juice, a piece of fruit, some muesli and a pot of vanilla yoghurt.

Tray loaded, he turned to scan the room and saw that Margaret had beaten him to it, having virtually finished her own breakfast already, or so it appeared.

'Morning!' he said with a bright smile as he approached the table where she was sitting. 'You're up early. Not sleep well? Strange little hotel, isn't it? I had the narrowest of beds. You?'

Lowering the cup of coffee from which she'd been sipping, she answered his morning brightness with a wry nod.

'Not that we can complain, I don't suppose,' he continued, sitting opposite her. 'Not that sort of a trip.' He began transferring his breakfast from tray to table. 'Any idea what delights today might have in store for you?'

'Why me?'

'Well, we are in Rome, no? The notice on the back of my bedroom door is in Italian so I naturally assumed...'

She cut him short with another wry nod. 'And it'll be Paris next,' she said. 'Just you wait. All those bars you mentioned.'

He shrugged. 'I only remember their names because I've never actually been to any of them.'

'Really? You haven't? But it's so close. Only a train ride away. Almost on the doorstep.'

'I know, I know. Something's always held me back though.'

'Scared of what you might find?'

'I guess.'

She grimaced. 'Well, if it's any consolation, I'm apprehensive too. About today. Because Switzerland certainly threw up some surprises and although they weren't too bad in the end, far from it, they still were...' She paused. 'Well, like I say, surprising. A lot to get one's poor old head around.'

He peeled back the lid of his yoghurt and then, when she didn't continue, prompted her by saying: 'To do with Simon, I suppose?'

'Simon and a whole lot besides.'

From her tone, he could tell she didn't care to elaborate, so he let the matter drop. She returned to sipping her coffee. He spooned some yoghurt into his mouth. Their silence was not uncompanianable.

'Mind you, to an extent we're all guilty in that regard,' he said eventually. 'We all have stories we like to tell ourselves and often they don't tally with reality.'

Again she nodded. 'Solace,' she agreed. 'We stand in need of constant solace.'

'It's only human.'

'Solace and guidance. That above all perhaps.'

At which juncture, as if on cue, the person whose job it was to lead them through their day appeared, unnoticed, in the doorway. Unnoticed because both Margaret and Geoffrey were too caught up in their respective thoughts. Cody looked appraisingly at the pair of them. Two heads nodding in agreement. Then he saw Geoffrey extend an unobtrusive hand and touch Margaret lightly on the arm. He expected her to stiffen. Interestingly, however, she didn't. Coolly, she just lifted her arm away in order to bring her cup of coffee to her lips once more.

Ever since his text exchange with Cedric, Cody had been weighing options for the day ahead. The possibilities were endless and he was still undecided. But now the sight of his two charges in such close communion made the decision for him and it was in a resolved state of mind that, a few moments later, he marched up to their table with some breakfast of his own.

'Morning!'

'Morning!'

'Morning!'

Cody set down his tray. 'No Simon?'

'Not yet,' sighed Margaret. 'I imagine the last two days have taken it out of him rather – I know they have me – and he always did need his sleep, poor lamb, even at the best of times. I did warn you, remember! Do you want me to fetch him?'

'No need,' said Cody. 'We're not in any hurry. The tickets are good all day.'

'Tickets? For what?' Margaret sounded taken aback; a little affronted even.

'I'm not forgetting,' said Cody quickly, 'that you'll have specific things you want to see and do, it being your choice of city. But just to get us going, I thought it would help to have some things arranged in advance.'

'Me, I need all the guidance you can offer,' grinned Geoffrey. 'A total virgin, me, when it comes to the eternal city.'

'Tickets for what?' demanded Margaret again.

'I thought the Doria Pamphilj Gallery.'

'The Doria Pamphilj?'

'You must know it?'

There was a freighted pause.

'The name,' conceded Margaret finally, without breaking eye contact. 'I know its reputation, of course I do, and the name. But it was actually one of the few places we didn't get to see that week. How clever of you to guess.' She continued to stare intently at Cody.

'I do my best,' said their guide.

'More coffee anyone?' asked Geoffrey, leaning across for the pot. 'Margaret? And *zucchero*?'

Margaret shook her head emphatically.

'There's quite a story associated with the Pamphilj family,' said Cody, turning to Geoffrey. 'The sort any writer might kill for. I'm sure you'll be fascinated.'

'Well, like I say,' replied Geoffrey, 'not knowing Rome in the slightest, I'm more than happy to go wherever you suggest. To me it's all fascinating. Aha! At last! The prodigal!' He gestured to where a sleepy-looking Simon was standing over the covered dishes at one end of the buffet, debating what sort of eggs to have.

Cody looked at his watch. 'Excellent!' he beamed. 'How about we gather in the lobby in, say, three quarters of an hour? That should give our late-comer more than enough time in which to scoff his breakfast.'

***

The Doria Pamphilj Gallery was just half an hour's walk from their hotel, with something to admire every step of the way. In the near distance, they glimpsed the cut-off outline of the Colosseum; there were gardens of palm and pine to wander through; buildings all around of every era, predominantly coloured in shades (yellow to deep brown) of ochre; and, as they neared the Piazza Venezia, a particularly grand mingling of the ages: Trajan's column coming into view first, with its spiralling frieze, then the white marble sweep of the monument to Victor Emmanuel II, pompously crowned at either end by horse-drawn chariots of bronze.

Along with the others, Margaret was of course taking note. How could she not? Rome demanded your attention. Although ever since those vignettes from her past had so vividly reminded her of the dilemma she faced – what to say; how to say it; when and where? – she'd been feeling more than usually on edge and it was only by a considerable effort of will that she was now able to make an appropriate quip as they gathered at the monument's base to gawp at its marbled prodigality.

'The wedding cake!' she said brightly. 'That's what they call it, some of the people. And you can understand why.'

'Or the typewriter,' added Cody, looking slyly at Geoffrey. 'Another nickname.'

'And over there?' asked Simon, indicating the long, straight and relatively narrow street that led away from the piazza on its other side. 'Where does that take you?'

'That's the Via del Corso,' said Cody. 'Famous for its shopping. And where we'll also find the Doria Pamphilj. Not far now.'

The stone facade of their destination, although grand (the arched entrance was wide enough to drive a coach through and there were a great many balconied and shuttered windows running the length of each of its three storeys), was as nothing compared to the interior. Here sumptuous high-ceilinged room followed sumptuous high-ceilinged room in an uninterrupted flow of baroque gilt, marble, glass, marquetry and red plush. There was no end either to the richness of the gallery's paintings. Brueghel, Caravaggio, Titian – you name it, the Doria Pamphilj family owned it. There was an immediately recognisable portrait by Velazquez of Pope Innocent X, himself a Pamphilj, and a double portrait by Margaret's favourite, Raphael. Although, as Geoffrey couldn't help noticing, she chose not to linger over this. Then came the palace apartments and, by the time they emerged onto the Via del Corso again – finding it busier than when they'd entered the gallery; the day's shoppers were out in force, tourists ditto, and the pavement was crammed – they were more than happy to fall in with Cody's suggestion that after a short walk to the Piazza Navona, they find themselves an outside café where they could relax for a bit.

'It's a beautiful square,' said Cody. 'One of the city's finest. We can have something to drink, maybe a bite, and...'

'You can tell us,' instructed Geoffrey, 'more about the family Pamphilj, please.' Thanks to what they'd learned during their gallery visit, he pronounced the 'j' as an 'i' – Pamphili. 'Yesterday I couldn't even have said the name right, let alone tell you anything of their history. When it comes to old popes, the Borgias are about as far as yours truly ever got.'

'So!' declared Cody, once they'd found themselves a table at the northern end of the Piazza Navona, opposite the fountain of Neptune, and a waiter had taken their order. 'The Pamphilj!' A pair of green eyes swept over his listeners. 'Like the Borgias, they were a papal family, which is what allowed them to accrue so much wealth, have so much influence. Two popes, lots of nepotism, lots of loot. There's another palazzo, also fine, at the other end of this square, which we can look at afterwards if you'd like. And when they married into more wealth from Genoa – that's the Doria lot – their power only increased. Though what interests people more these days, I have to say, is the current generation.'

They'd ordered coffees and beers and something light to eat, which Cody now seasoned with a spicy account of the latest in the Doria Pamphilj saga. It started, he said, after World War Two, when the family's sole heir, a princess, who was working at the time for the Catholic Women's League, met and married a British naval officer. Unable to produce children of their own – or at least this is what Cody guessed to be the reason – the couple adopted, from England, a daughter and a son. The former grew up to marry another Catholic, an art historian, with whom she had four daughters. While the son, who runs the family estate, turned out to be gay; although this didn't deter him and his civil partner – they'd cemented their union under UK law, explained Cody – from following in his parents' footsteps and adopting a son of their own, also a daughter.

'And here's where it gets complicated,' said Cody.

As a particularly staunch Catholic, the adopted children's aunt decided to challenge their right to any share of the family fortune by citing the fact that Italian law doesn't or didn't recognise either civil partnerships or surrogate motherhood. In her eyes, the adopted children might just as well have been illegitimate. More or less were, indeed. Half persons. So lawyers were summoned and the ensuing case stretched over a number of years, with the inevitable result that any affection there'd ever been between brother and sister totally evaporated. Two vastly differing belief systems had come into conflict and although the case was eventually thrown out, the scars it must have left...

'Well, I don't imagine,' concluded Cody, 'that they'll ever quite heal. Apparently brother and sister both have apartments in the palazzo, but is there any coming and going between the two establishments? Personally, I doubt it. Maybe in time – who knows! – things will change. When the younger generation take over. One can only hope. But for now...' He left the sentence unfinished.

'Wow!' said Geoffrey; and again he made use of a word of Simon's. 'Awesome! Never mind Bruno's family story, this one knocks that into a cocked hat. A novel and a half, this is. Fabulous wealth, sibling rivalry, differing belief systems. Has it all. Sure to sell millions.'

'In which case,' said Cody, 'for when you're good and ready, why not?'

Before Geoffrey could reply, however, Margaret had pushed back her chair and was rising swiftly to her feet. In response to the earlier family saga, she'd somehow managed (or so she thought) to wipe away her tears without the others noticing. This time she wasn't so fortunate.

'Auntie M?' Simon, who'd been lost in contemplation of the well-muscled statue of Neptune in the fountain opposite, looked up worriedly.

Geoffrey spoke too. 'Something wrong?'

'Sorry!' said Margaret. 'I'm afraid that being here again is having more of an impact than I'd bargained for. Too many memories and I think I need to be on my own for a bit, if you don't mind. Sorry, Simon. You go on without me. I can always find my own way back later. Let's meet at the hotel. Shall we?

Some time alone and I'll be fine, just fine.' Then she snatched up her bag and headed blindly for the piazza's centre.

As the crowd swallowed her up, Geoffrey coughed lightly and said: 'Simon, shouldn't you perhaps...?'

But he got no further because Cody interrupted with: 'If anyone goes after her, I think it should be you, Geoffrey.'

'Me? Really?'

The two men regarded each other. Then Cody said quietly: '*Sant'Agnese in Agone*, I think you'll find.'

'Beg your pardon?'

'That church over there, the one opposite Bernini's big fountain. Which, incidentally, he designed for Pope Innocent X. The dove with an olive twig in its beak on the top of the obelisk is the Pamphilj family emblem. Another detail for that putative novel perhaps. But anyway! *Sant'Agnese in Agone*. That's where I'd start.'

Frowningly, Geoffrey looked from Simon to Cody and back again.

'Don't worry,' said Cody. 'We'll wait here. Won't go anywhere without you. Will we, Simon?'

'This is all so weird,' said Geoffrey, standing up. 'Weird, weird, weird!'

As he moved off, Cody leaned forward and said quietly: 'I hope you don't think she went off because of you? Because yesterday, on the boat, I couldn't help noticing how she held you after you'd spoken to her. Tight, like she didn't want to let you go. Not ever.'

'Actually, I'm not so sure,' said Simon. 'You think the Doria Pamphilj gang take the cake? Our family has its demons too. Wrong word, but still.' His expression darkened. 'Where has she just gone, did you say? Exactly! Into the nearest church. Religion creeps in everywhere. My parents were the same.' He smiled crookedly. 'Well, not the same at all, in fact. They were evangelicals. Happy clappers. But it makes no difference.

Happy clapping. Catholicism. Name me a religion that doesn't disapprove of those who fail to conform!'

'Or maybe,' suggested Cody, 'maybe what you told her has triggered something that she now feels she must tell you in exchange? But doesn't know how.'

Again the crooked smile. 'Auntie M lost for words? You can't be serious!'

'You think that's impossible?'

There was a considered pause.

Then Simon said, in a more neutral tone: 'No, I guess you're right. She *was* amazing yesterday. Given what I had to tell her. She's always been so supportive. The best aunt ever. Unlike my parents, because I can't even begin to imagine what it would have been like with them. No, Auntie M, for all her hang-ups, is cut from a different cloth. And it's not as if she doesn't have certain other things she feels she must worry about. Like how I work for Malcolm at the garden centre, for instance, instead of being sensible and going to uni.'

'Though that sounds to me,' put in Cody, 'like quite a fine place to be. All things considered. Growing plants – I wouldn't mind myself.'

'You like gardening?'

'Sure I do. Or, to be accurate, let's say the thought of having one, because in my line of work it's kind of impossible, I'm away too much. But one day – fingers crossed! Hopefully one day!'

'Well, it's certainly a lovely thing, to be around gardens. I find it very – sustaining.' Simon's smile had lost its crookedness. 'I even suppose,' he continued, somewhat dreamily, 'that I could maybe go to university and study them. That might be a possibility. Keep my pernickety old aunt happy that way. Plant science. Why not?'

'So much to decide upon!' said Cody. 'But choices are good. It's when you don't have choice that you need to start worrying.' He found that he was smiling too. 'And isn't it nice,' he went on, 'to be in such a beautiful square? On a day like this, in the summer sun and in the best of company.'

'Couldn't be nicer!' assented Simon. If it was at all odd to him that Cody should know, or appear to know, pretty much all that had passed between himself and Auntie M on the boat, he didn't let this ruffle the contentment that was stealing over him. In fact, he welcomed Cody's omnipotence and, as his eyes drifted again to where the well-muscled figure of Neptune was wrestling in stone with a coiled octopus whose tentacles were tightly wrapped around Neptune's straining thighs, his smile became quite radiant.

***

Cody had guessed right. Margaret was in *Sant'Agnese in Agone*. Where, since Simon had also hit the nail on the head regarding religion and how it crept in everywhere, she was pondering her Catholicism.

As children, neither she nor Susan had given God much thought, except perhaps to sneer at their parents' brand of wish-washy Anglicism. Her mother's quaint insistence on wearing a hat to church on those few occasions (high days and holidays) when she did attend. Her father's concomitant reluctance to accompany his wife. But then Henry had appeared on the scene and, for Susan at least, everything had changed. She would hang on Henry's every word as he explained how revelatory it had been for him when a friend had introduced him to his church; and soon Susan was experiencing just such a Damascene moment herself, as orchestrated by her new boyfriend. Which at the time had only strengthened Margaret in her own mistrust of religion. Where Susan went, Margaret didn't care to follow. Thank you very much!

But God moves in mysterious ways and, in Buenos Aires, Margaret would eventually experience a Damascene moment too. Her flat was on the top floor, with a view of rooftops and, in the distance, a solid church tower where a bell would toll at various hours of the day. And it was while standing at the window early one morning, looking across this dawn-tinged panorama, that the bell had struck and amazingly, unavoidably, she'd known it to be ringing for her above all others.

So, without further thought, she'd run downstairs, found her way to the solid church and slipped inside it to sit through her first morning mass.

Of course, there'd been other factors in play as well. It wasn't only the tolling of a bell. There was Gustavo and everything that had happened in Rome, where she'd also been drawn into a church once; the one with the gaudily got up Virgin Mary. Rome and then all of afterwards. The whole painful mess; her distress; her unstoppable tears. All had rendered her supremely vulnerable, which in some eyes – even her own at times – could make one question the entire experience. God nabbing you just because you were down. But then you thought: flesh is by its nature weak and what shame is there ultimately in acknowledging this fact and asking for His help? Isn't that why He's with us in the first place? To offer sanctuary. Shelter from the storm. Some certainty.

Except that in the light of what Cody had just done, canny operator that he was, sanctuary and certainty – even in this most baroque of churches in the heart of the eternal city, with its elaborately fashioned walls and ceiling, its many arches and vast dome, its gilt and opulence, its pillared high altar, all the trappings of celestial reassurance – even here sanctuary and certainty currently felt wholly out of reach. Since Cody had not only taken them to the very gallery where Gustavo had first stood her up, but had then used it as a pretext for telling a story with particularly painful and bitter resonances. Nor was it just the obvious parallels. How religion could be used to drive a wedge between siblings. Or how the whole question of homosexuality was one that any Catholic must wrestle with. Although, in actual fact, she didn't feel that this was too much of a problem for her. Whatever Simon was, she would support him. Of course she would. And would take more care in future too to ensure her Catholicism didn't come between them. She could see how her beliefs might have made him hold back in the past. Caused him to fear her reaction. She wasn't blind.

But this was almost by the by when it came to the story which she herself must now tell. Beginning, she supposed, since this is what Cody's Roman itinerary had subliminally suggested, beginning with the time Gustavo had first stood her up. Although in order to have even the faintest chance of doing this, and doing it successfully, first she must pray. Demand the guidance that suddenly seemed so very out of reach. The guidance and the succour. The strength. All that He could provide. All that she so desperately needed.

Normally, she had little difficulty asking for divine help. But today, as she sank to her knees and put her hands together and lowered her head, today she found that the words simply wouldn't come.

She glanced up and who should be hovering at the end of the pew? An awkward-looking Geoffrey, that's who! His battered leather bag hung uncomfortably from one shoulder, pulling his T-shirt out of alignment and allowing her a glimpse of hairy stomach. His spiky grey hair could have done with a comb too. But behind their heavy frames, his dark eyes remained steady, like those of a story-book owl.

'May I?' Depositing his bag on the pew, he sat alongside it. So she sat also and, for a drawn-out moment, there was silence. Then he said, very softly: 'I don't mean to pry or be presumptuous, but you did seem pretty upset back there and I was worried. We all were.'

'So Cody suggested you come looking for me. Is that how this goes?'

'You don't think I'd be capable of deciding for myself?' He paused. Then, eyes still on her, he went on: 'What, Margaret, what? Cody tells us about some aristocratic Roman family I've never even heard of and you run away. I noticed in Switzerland too, when Bruno told us his family story, how upset you became then. There were tears in your eyes on that occasion also.'

So – she'd not gone unobserved after all on that terrace! She looked towards the distant altar; the green marble pillars to either side of the white marble centrepiece; the ornate gold capital and arched cluster of little angels that crowned it; the gold candlesticks; the gold tabernacle in the very centre of all that pomp for holding the simple host. And again there were tears in her eyes.

'Okay,' she said finally, voice low. 'Much like Bruno, much like Cody, I too have a family story to tell. Although, in my case, I don't know where or when or how to bloody well start. It isn't easy.'

'A common writer's complaint,' countered Geoffrey smoothly. 'So what you have to do is plunge straight in. Start with me, why don't you? I'm a good listener. All ears. And still no joke intended.'

She looked assessively into that steady pair of eyes.

'Go on,' he said. 'I dare you!'

So, without further demur, she started with Rome and the art trip. Their cheap *pensione*, the other giggling girls, a guide called Gustavo, who – *inter alia* – had promised to take her separately to the Doria Pamphilj Gallery to see the Raphael there, among its many treasures.

'But this morning you said you'd never been!'

'Because the bastard stood me up, didn't he! And I should have known then, it was a sort of sign, but fool that I was, I preferred to ignore what was staring me in the face.'

'Woah! Not so fast!' Geoffrey held up an admonishing hand. 'One thing to plunge straight in, but until I cotton on, you do need to take this at less of a lick.'

More gradually, therefore, and with fewer ellipses, she told him about standing with Gustavo in front of Raphael's *La Fornarina*; their first drink in a bar near the *pensione* where she was staying; visiting his apartment; how he'd painted her portrait. Everything she could bear to share.

'And then he stood you up, you say? Bastard indeed!'

'Just the once and he did have an excuse, so at the time – well, it was easy to fool myself. I didn't really think anything of it, truth be told. Not then.'

'And afterwards?'

'Afterwards I flew home. The trip was over.'

'But this, I'm guessing, is nevertheless how you ended up in Buenos Aires. Yes?'

Here Margaret came to a complete halt, however, the look on her face one of such unutterable despair that had Geoffrey not known better, he would have put his arms around her. As it was, he didn't even dare lay a consoling hand on her arm. Not even briefly. He just sat there, waiting on her next utterance.

'I've been such a coward,' she said at last, gazing altar-wards. 'In all sorts of ways. A terrible, terrible coward. You get into the habit and then you don't know how to do things differently. Until you can't escape yourself.' She turned to face him. 'I know you've started me off,' she continued in a near whisper. 'For which I'm really grateful. Believe me. But this is about as far as I can go right now. Let's rejoin the others, shall we? And tomorrow – well, by tomorrow things may perhaps be a little clearer. Anything's possible, with Cody at the helm.'

'He certainly likes to keep one on one's toes!' Rising, Geoffrey slung his bag over his shoulder once more. 'Right then! The other two will still be at our table I think. They promised they wouldn't move.'

After the hush of the church, the sunlit square represented a sensory assault, both aural and visual. People everywhere, going to and fro, loud chatter and laughter, car engines revving, scooters whining, water splashing in Bernini's central fountain. A man with an accordion had started to play at a spot not far from their table, something old style and cheesy – "Three Coins in the Fountain", was that it? Margaret knew the tune but wasn't sure of the name – and Cody and Simon were listening to the wheezy music with a shared smile on their rapt faces. They looked good together, Margaret thought. Cody a dazzle of white in the sun, golden hair ablaze too (his red cap having been discarded); with Simon sitting prudently in the shade of the overhead umbrella, one demure foot tapping quietly away in time to the jaunty music.

'Ah!' said Cody, looking up. 'There you both are! We were wondering. Tell you what: time for another photo, wouldn't you say?' He fumbled in his pocket for his phone. 'Pity to be in this most glorious of squares on such a sunny day without somehow marking the occasion.'

Day 5

After Cody had finished photographing the three of them, which he did while also managing to include the accordion player in the background, he'd fumbled in his pocket again, this time for surprise tickets to the Borghese Gallery.

'You'll have gone of course on your first visit,' he'd said to Margaret; all innocence. 'Everyone does. But the others haven't and I can't imagine you'd have much objection to going again all these years on. Then afterwards we could walk in those lovely gardens. Simon will like that.'

'If you insist,' she'd said. 'Stir up as many memories as you can, why don't you!'

Although there were shifts in perspective, she found, second time around, useful shifts – never mind that she'd been the one to choose Rome in the first place; she couldn't blame Cody for that – and, as she emerged from sleep the next morning to find they were still very much there (same narrow bed; same cell-like room), her waking thoughts were more to do – for a while at least – with the present than with the past. Like how it had felt to be standing before *La Fornarina* again, with Geoffrey by her side on this occasion, unconsciously echoing her earlier companion by saying: 'Looks like this might be another of your favourites. Is it, Margaret? One very sexy lady, whatever the case.'

To which she'd not immediately replied. Only at dinner, which they'd eaten in a small trattoria just around the corner from their hotel, had she found an answer (of sorts) by telling him that nothing was how it seemed. Not even Raphael. She wasn't sure when she'd learned this – she hadn't known it in her youth, that's for sure – but the painting in the Borghese Gallery was only a copy of the original, which hung in the Palazzo Barberini. An excellent copy, but still a copy.

'Surfaces,' she said, 'can be cruelly deceptive.'

'What's that, Auntie M?' Simon, on the opposite side of the table, was apparently finding the little trattoria too noisy for ease of conversation. He'd leaned forward in order to pose the question.

'Not important.'

'Your well-versed aunt,' explained Geoffrey, leaning forward also, 'is giving me a lesson in art appreciation.'

'Oh, is that what this is?'

'And she certainly knows a thing or two,' persevered Geoffrey, ignoring Margaret's interjection. 'Puts the rest of us well and truly in the shade.'

'You can say that again!' agreed Simon zestfully.

But did she, though? Put anyone anywhere? Because even by the light of a fresh day, she still had no handle on the most crucial thing of all: how to screw up her courage to the point where she could properly start telling Simon all that she must. Starting – since this much had at least been decided in her mind – with the carefully selected memory of what it had been like to stand alone in the Piazza Venezia below the steps to that vulgar monument as she waited on Gustavo, who'd chosen this as an obvious place to rendezvous, it being only a short walk from the Doria Pamphilj Gallery, which he'd promised to show her separately at the end of the day since it hadn't been on the official itinerary and was, he said, one of Roma's best.

But then, with Gustavo, every damn gallery was 'one of Roma's best'. It was to a large degree what she so liked about him. The generosity of his spirit. His grinning enthusiasm. The ready flash of those teeth.

But that afternoon, as she soon discovered, there'd been precious little to admire in his behaviour. She'd waited over an hour in the piazza, watching other tourists come and go and having more than once to offer her services as photographer to happy couples who wanted their picture taken against the marble background of the monument. Until she'd returned in despair to the *pensione* for supper – and still no sign of him! Only much later, as she'd been getting ready for bed, had the concierge – a woman in her sixties with arthritic hips – come complainingly up the stairs to tell her that she was wanted on the phone in the lobby.

On a hopelessly crackly line, with the words being regularly and brutally truncated or hissed over, Gustavo explained that his elderly aunt (his father's older sister, she gathered, who happened to live in Rome) had been the problem. Her cat was sick and he'd had to take them to the vet because now that he was in Rome too, his aunt tended to rely on him in emergencies. Or that's what Margaret understood him to be saying, at any rate. The nature of the line precluded certainty.

Then he said, and this she did hear, that tomorrow he would be around again – *seguro* – and before she could tell him not to bother, with a final crackle, the line went dead. And when he did appear the next day, early, while they were still finishing breakfast, it was with such an extravagant bunch of flowers that continued hurt and anger were impossible. Besides, the other girls in their group were watching jealously.

So here was her starting point. But to then proceed to the next stage? *Plunge straight in*, Geoffrey had urged. Easier said than done, however, and did she have it in her? She hadn't yesterday.

Swinging out of bed at last, she put her feet to the reassuring firmness of the cool tiled floor. And, as she did this, so it came to her in a revelatory flash. Of course! For what had Geoffrey also said? *Start with me, why don't you? I'm a good listener. All ears.* Yes, she would, she must continue to use Geoffrey. Practise her story, but all of it, soup to nuts, on him beforehand, preparing herself incrementally for the greater task of telling Simon afterwards. Plunge in, yes, but do it in stages, testing the water as she went by tracing, for Geoffrey's inquisitive ears alone initially, Gustavo's many abandonments, minor to major.

***

Cody was faced, as he awoke, with a not dissimilar conundrum to Margaret's: how best to plan their second day in Rome? The Friday hadn't been a failure exactly, but if he wanted to tick all the necessary boxes, things should have progressed quite a bit further than they actually had. And time was finite too. Just two or three more days. That's all he had left.

In the shower, he ran through various possibilities. None that grabbed him, however. Until, as he was putting on a clean T-shirt, the memory of how easy it had been to get Geoffrey to go looking for Margaret in *Sant'Agnese in Agone* – that and how they had looked together on returning from the church, which is what had inspired him to take the photograph – made him decide that what he should do was engineer it for the two of them to spend the morning alone together. That should solve the problem. Although if he did do this, then what about Simon?

Running a quick comb through his hair, he double checked the mirror to see how he was looking.

To his surprise, he was the last to arrive at breakfast, where he also found that the day was already in hand.

'Sleep badly?' asked Geoffrey as Cody set down his tray.

'No, I slept just fine,' said Cody, pulling out a chair. 'Why?'

'You look a little tired,' said Geoffrey, 'is all. But then having us lot to worry about can't be easy. So I hope you'll be relieved to hear that Margaret and I have decided to look after ourselves this morning, for a change. If that's okay?'

'You see,' said Margaret, looking up from her coffee, 'I'd really like to find some of the places from last time I was here. In essence, a trip down memory lane, which would be too, too boring for you and Simon. As I'm sure you'll both agree. Is that all right, Simon, dear?'

'Whereas yours truly doesn't mind a little boredom,' chuckled Geoffrey. 'And Margaret *has* expressed a desire for some company at least.'

Cody glanced towards Simon, who was in the act of buttering some toast. 'So in that case,' he said, 'any idea what you might like to do?'

Simon looked up. 'Well, I really liked those gardens yesterday. If there are any more of those to be had. What do you reckon?'

Cody considered. 'Rome's pretty built up,' he said, 'but I'm sure we can find something. If we look hard enough.'

Margaret clapped her hands. 'Perfect!' she cried. 'Everything sorted.'

'Well, in part.' There was a mock frown on Geoffrey's face.

'What?' asked Margaret, perplexed. Then, having noticed the direction of Geoffrey's gaze, her face softened. 'Oh,' she said, smiling, 'of course. You're needing the... what is it again? *Zucchero?*'

'Can't help it,' grinned Geoffrey, 'if I have a sweet tooth. Can I now?'

***

When Geoffrey joined Margaret a little later in the lobby, she'd a fold-out map in one hand for the purpose of pointing out to him the areas that wanted revisiting.

'There,' she said, 'and there and there and there. If you're really sure about tagging along?'

'Of course I am!' he confirmed as they set off in the direction of Trastevere. 'Delighted to be asked.' They went past the café on the corner of the square. 'Apart from anything else, it gives me the opportunity to ask you more about yourself. You've told me a little about your earlier trip to Rome, but before that? Or afterwards? Hardly anything.'

Goodness! thought Margaret. *At this rate, formulating and then practising my story on you might actually prove less difficult than imagined. You'll have it out of me in next to no time!*

Or was that wishful thinking? One thing to have an avid listener walking by your side; quite another to shape the narrative coherently, give the events their required weight, find words for what had, until now, proved entirely impossible to say.

'I don't even know where you lived in those days, or where you were studying,' continued Geoffrey. 'Do we turn right here?'

Margaret consulted the map. 'Yes, then a left.'

The route she'd chosen took them along a number of cobbled back streets, wide enough only for a single car once you'd factored in the parked vehicles that were tucked at every angle into every available space. Although at intervals these streets would also connect with wider avenues or sudden squares or patches of open ground and there were always churches or grander mansions or remnants of ancient Rome to draw the eye. Nothing was without the sheen of history.

'So?' invited Geoffrey. 'Home was...?'

'Suffolk,' said Margaret. 'The same village it's always been. Outside Ipswich. Small, sleepy, quite picturesque, but nothing out of the ordinary. In fact, if you wanted one word to describe our village, that would have to be it. Ordinary. Thoroughly ordinary.'

'And your parents? Were they from there originally?'

Margaret hadn't thought to go back this far; but it was, she supposed, all part of her tale; and approaching the denouement step by slow step was no bad thing either. So:

Yes, both parents were Suffolk-born, she said; father a post office clerk; mother a housewife; keen dancers in their youth, the two of them, which is how they'd met, at some local hop; although they'd not actually married until Margaret had come along and by then the dancing had stopped; home a council house on the edge of the village that they'd later been able to buy; one sister, younger, called Susan; the one who'd married Henry and then been killed in the car crash.

'The born agains!' exclaimed Geoffrey, who'd not forgotten. 'If it's okay to be calling them that?'

'It's what they were.'

'And you're a horse of a different colour. Or at least, I think that's how you described yourself.'

'Catholic, yes.'

'So how did that happen? I don't suppose it can have been your parents?'

'Heavens no! It was BA. Buenos Aires.'

'Aha! The Gustavo connection!'

'To an extent.'

They'd come to a T-junction and Margaret needed to consult the map again. Geoffrey studied her bowed head; the pleasing fact that her hair was actually silvery rather than merely grey, and very fine, as if spun from metallic gossamer. She really was a most attractive woman. Then she looked up and the expression in her eyes put him in mind of the clear distress he'd seen there yesterday in that church, when the subject of Buenos Aires and Gustavo had first arisen. Better not to push things, he thought. Stay with Suffolk. Although there was in fact no need for him to steer the conversation anywhere. Margaret did that for him.

'No,' she was saying, 'if we ever went to church as children, it was only at Christmas. Maybe Easter at a pinch. So it was quite a shock when Susan told us about Henry and how she'd rushed to join his church. Which she did, can you believe, on the evening of my return from Rome. When all I wanted to talk about was all of this.' She gestured at the elegant building they happened to be passing. 'Bloody upstager!'

'From your tone,' said Geoffrey, 'I gather it wasn't just religion which you and your sister didn't see eye to eye over?'

'Spot on,' allowed Margaret, eyes on the building still.

'May one ask why?'

'She was very prickly as a character. Had a definite chip on her shoulder. Jealousy, I suppose. In essence.'

'Of you, you mean?'

Margaret nodded. 'Usual younger sibling stuff. She thought I always got my own way and that she never did. I was our parents' favourite. Blah-blah. I'd been given the looks and the brains. I could do no wrong. Except in her eyes, of course. There I could do no right.' Her voice had tightened.

'If you'd rather not talk about any of this,' said Geoffrey, 'you must please just say. I always was too nosy for my own good.'

'No, no!' Now Margaret sounded almost frantic. 'It's fine to be talking. I don't often get the chance. And I do need to...' Here she broke off, although not before Geoffrey had instinctively guessed what she'd been about to say next. Practise! *And I do need to practise.* That's how he imagined she'd meant to end her sentence.

Except why would she need to be practising? And on him, of all people?

The river came into view, and the Ponte Sublicio, with its surprisingly leafy outlook for somewhere so close to the city centre.

'Pause here?' suggested Geoffrey. 'I could do with a breather. Take in the view for a bit. The legendary Tiber, etcetera, etcetera. Your sister should have known better than to be upstaging you when you had all of this at your fingertips to talk about. What they missed!'

'I know,' said Margaret. 'I know.'

They were motionless for a while, lost in contemplation of the bucolic scene: a bridge, water, trees. Then Margaret cleared her throat and took up her story again. She spoke of the speed with which Susan and Henry had become an item. Speed all round, in fact. A mere six weeks until the shock of their father leaving home and walking out of their lives forever. Their mother's cancer diagnosis. Susan and Henry's hasty marriage. Standing between the two of them at the crematorium as their mother's coffin disappeared from view. Another forever.

'I'm beginning to understand,' said Geoffrey, 'why you might have wanted to get away to Argentina.'

Which was as good a prompt as any for what must inevitably follow. Except that right now she needed another pause in order to gather her thoughts and be sure of approaching the final moment in the correct manner, slow and steady.

'Yes, well,' she said, 'BA – a whole raft of things motivated my move there. *And* my eventual return after Susan and Henry were killed. But before I go into all of that, because it's all very complicated, complicated in the extreme, why don't we stop somewhere for a coffee? There's a place I have in mind near where I once stayed. Come!'

They crossed the river and walked into the open area where, as Margaret then began explaining, there was a famous flea market on Sundays; an area overlooked by the white stone facade of the old city gate of Porta Portese.

'The flea market,' said Margaret, whose pace had quickened; she was now marginally ahead of Geoffrey, 'is right here, more or less. Although we didn't actually get to see it, I have to say, just heard about it; there wasn't time. And through the large gate over there, that's Trastevere. Our old stomping ground.'

Because she was ahead of him, Geoffrey couldn't help but notice how she stiffened on saying this, much as an animal might, sensing danger. He looked about them, but saw nothing of note. Except perhaps for a well-preserved man in a summer suit coming through the ancient gate towards them, taking care all the while to keep out of the way of the cars that also came sweeping through it. Once clear of the gate, the man paused and looked behind him to where a younger woman was taking equal care to avoid the traffic, not least because she was holding the hand of a girl dressed all in blue. Either the man's daughter and granddaughter, surmised Geoffrey; or else a much younger (trophy?) wife.

Meanwhile, Margaret had turned aside and was saying urgently: 'Careful of the traffic! These Roman drivers...'

'What?' he demanded. 'What's wrong?' He could instantly tell that something pretty serious – more than mere traffic – must have occurred. 'What, Margaret, what?'

'I think it's him,' she whispered. 'In fact, I'm sure of it. Bloody Cody and his damn tricks!'

Under normal circumstances, Geoffrey might have needed more than a mere 'him' to be put in the picture. But as it was...

'I thought,' he said, 'at least I assumed, that Gustavo was in Buenos Aires? Or are you suggesting he might have moved to Italy?'

'Why ask me?'

'Who else would I ask?'

'It's years and years, another life, since we were in touch.'

'And the woman?'

Margaret began to cry. 'You think I know that either!' Then she threw back her head and turned to fully face the man who, while they'd been talking, had waited for the woman with the girl to catch up with him and now had a proprietorial arm around her waist. They couldn't have been more than ten yards away, fifteen at most, and Geoffrey and Margaret were directly in their path; yet the man appeared not to see them, being wholly focused on the woman by his side, who was bending down as she walked because the girl was asking her something. And so, smiling and talking together, the compact trio went past without so much as glancing at either onlooker.

'The woman?' snorted Margaret. 'I've not the faintest. Though I will say this: there never was any shortage of women in Gustavo's life. Sorry! Don't mean to sound bitter, but that's the truth of it.'

Geoffrey swivelled round for one last look at the trio. Simultaneously, the man looked back too, as if he'd only that moment become aware of having been observed. His eyes, which were darkly alert, found Geoffrey's and – unexpectedly; flagrantly – he winked. Then he pulled the woman more securely towards him, planting a lingering kiss on her forehead as he did so.

Geoffrey checked to see whether Margaret had noticed. Apparently not, which was just as well. Rather, she was facing the other way, towards the city gate.

'That coffee,' she said. 'I could really do with that coffee.'

They walked briskly on, coming after a few blocks to a road sign that said: *Viale di Trastevere.*

'Which way now?' asked Geoffrey. 'Do you remember?'

'I think to the right first,' said Margaret. 'Then a left. The street with our *pensione* in it was somewhere off this one, but much narrower.'

They turned down a few much narrower streets before reaching the one required, where Margaret was able to recognise the *pensione* from the small red sign above its door.

'That's it!' she cried. 'Hasn't changed.' They stood looking up at the building. 'My room was at the top, but at the back. No view of the street, just a grubby little courtyard, piled high with crates.'

'Looks charming though,' said Geoffrey. 'From this angle.'

'And the bar I have in mind,' Margaret went on, 'is just around the corner.' She didn't add that this was the bar where she and Gustavo had gone on their first evening together. But then she didn't need to. As with the man in the summer suit, Geoffrey had already guessed.

There wasn't much to see through the bar's dirt-streaked window, except for a few tables and the outline of a counter running along the rear wall; yet it was enough to make Geoffrey wonder whether Margaret mightn't decide in the end to go somewhere a little less cramped and drab and dingy. They had after all passed a few attractive establishments in the last stages of their walk. But she pushed open the door regardless, making straight for a table towards the back of the room, set slightly apart, in a corner.

'What can I get you?' asked Geoffrey after they'd both pulled out chairs for themselves.

'Flat white?'

'Flat white coming up! And anything to nibble?'

She shook her head.

He placed their order at the bar with a dark-haired woman who, as with the waitress who'd served them in that lakeside town in Switzerland, once again looked not dissimilar to the Romanian who'd served them at breakfast in Amsterdam; although judging by her accent, this waitress could only be Italian.

'Two coffee,' she said, giving the words a signature flourish. 'And some water, *si?*'

'Thank you,' said Geoffrey. 'That would be lovely, yes. Thank you.'

'You sit, I bring.'

Returning to Margaret, whose head was lowered as she rummaged in her bag for something, he sat down and was about to make some jokey reference to the ongoing similarity between waitresses on this trip – how in Cody's world so much seemed stage-managed – when she looked up, causing any thoughts of Cody to vanish. All that counted was the liquid pain in her eyes.

'Heavens!' he said as she began blowing her nose on a crumpled tissue. 'Would you rather we were somewhere else? Because we can always just...'

Stuffing her tissue back into her bag, she smiled crookedly. 'Ah, but can we though?'

'Of course we can. We can go anywhere we like. Rome is our oyster. Yours, anyway.'

Vigorously, she shook her head. 'Rome is my nemesis, you mean.'

'I do?'

'Yes,' she said. 'Really.'

'In which case,' said Geoffrey quietly, 'you do also need to bear in mind that even the best of listeners must be given the complete story if they're to make complete sense of things. And so far, all I've been handed is snippets. Crucial ones, I'm sure, but even so.'

The waitress came up with a tray, on which she'd placed their coffees and two glasses of water.

'Right,' said Margaret after the waitress had withdrawn. 'Me and Gustavo.' She took a careful sip of water. 'The full story.'

As she spoke, Geoffrey's attention was caught by a shadowing at the window. A man was standing there, face pressed to the glass. None other indeed than the man in the summer suit, the one they'd passed by the Porta Portese. But seen more clearly in the window's frame. The iron-grey hair, the probing eyes and a set of film star teeth – the intensity with which he was staring through the glass was causing him to grimace – whose whiteness was made all the more vivid by the man's impressive tan.

Where was the younger woman, Geoffrey wondered? And the girl? Then he thought: no, not integral to Margaret, who had her back to the window thankfully and was repeating in a low yet determined voice: 'Right! The full story. As best and as fully as I damn well can.'

***

Cody hadn't meant for the name to recur, but in sussing out somewhere green for himself and Simon to head towards, the landscaped park abutting the seventeenth-century Villa Doria Pamphilj had seemed about the most promising. Not only was it large – Rome's largest, he read as he googled – but apparently it featured many appealing contrasts: hedged areas of formal design; expanses of sloping meadow; fountains and ponds; a lake and a canal; a scattering of architectural gems, some attractively ruined; and a great many paths for ease of access, some with benches on them so that when you were tired, you could rest. As Simon and Cody were doing now in fact, in a section of park overlooking a tranquil lawn.

'Personally, I'm not so into formal gardens,' Simon was saying of the stretch they'd just been through. 'All those clipped little hedges. Stunted-looking, I always think. Give me something shaggier, shaggier and wilder, any day.'

'That's because you're an Englishman,' offered Cody. 'It's the Europeans – the French and Italians especially – who favour the formal. But this you must already know.'

'I do remember reading once,' nodded Simon, 'about the Italians and their Renaissance ideals of order and harmony. Derived from ancient Rome, you know. The need to bring nature under control. As a final measure of what's actually civilised.'

'Unlike us bloody-minded Brits then,' sighed Cody, 'who like to promote a degree of disorder.'

Simon frowned. 'Brexit at every turn, hey, concealed in every leaf! No escaping destiny.'

A silence fell, during which they both sat staring at some remnants of crumbling masonry on the far side of the lawn, where presumably an entire building had once stood. Something whole, reduced by time to the merest shadow of a constituent part.

'Talking of destiny,' continued Simon pensively, 'if you were at all right yesterday, in that awesome square you took us to, when you said that maybe Auntie M, who like I say has been amazing, truly amazing, that maybe she now has something she wants to tell me....' But here he tailed off.

'Yes?' prompted Cody.

'I just wish I knew,' concluded Simon, 'what it was. That's all. Because until now, not a clue has been given. Absolutely zilch!' Again he frowned. 'Mind you, like I said then, our whole damn family... there are all sorts of no go areas. It's not just the God stuff. Like why, setting religion aside for a moment, did my mother and Auntie M not ever see eye to eye? She's never really said. Or what about my grandfather, come to that, their father? Who walked out one day, quite a thing I would have thought, yet she doesn't like to talk about that either. And now it's too late, of course. He's most probably dead. Or there's my uncle on my father's side, who went to live in New Zealand, my grandparents too, I think there must have been some sort of family schism there as well that's never been discussed.'

'Family stories!' murmured Cody. 'We've certainly had our fill these past few days. But I wouldn't worry. When she's good and ready, then you'll know. Some things take time. Can't be forced or hurried. And in the meantime...'

Here they were interrupted by a man with outstretched hands. Apparently of African origin – he'd a gleaming black skin – and clearly penniless, certainly if his clothing (oversized shorts, no shoes, a torn T-shirt) and posture were anything to go by. In a gesture that required no words of explanation, he brought the fingers of his right hand together, opened wide his mouth and raised his bunched fingers towards it. His dark eyes were beseeching.

Only then did he speak. '*Mangiare*,' he said in a hoarse voice. '*Mangiare*.'

Simon had no hard and fast rule about beggars. Sometimes he gave, sometimes he didn't; it all depended. But today he felt utterly impelled; although no sooner had he begun reaching for his wallet than he realised, of course, that he'd no change. Cody had been taking care of their finances.

'Oh, dear,' he said, half to the man in front of them, half to Cody. 'I'm afraid I...'

'That's all right,' said Cody. 'Here, let me.'

'You are English?' The supplicant sounded both surprised and, the stronger emotion perhaps, quite delighted. 'I go England. I have family. Oxford. Good city Oxford. England good country. Everyone like England.'

'These days?' Cody affected a look of some disbelief. 'Funnily enough, we've just touched on that very subject and I wouldn't be too sure.' He handed the man a note, then glanced at Simon. 'Hey?' he added. 'Given what we were saying earlier about Brexit and so forth.'

'It's such a long way too,' said Simon as the man thrust Cody's offering into a pocket. 'How on earth will you manage it?'

The beggar's English was limited, but he'd enough to outline his itinerary. He'd crossed into Italy from Libya and Sicily it seemed and was planning another sea crossing when he got to France, Calais being his ultimate destination there. A boat of some kind, he hoped. He had a name and he had a number. Then Oxford and his family. A distant cousin.

'Jesus wept!' said Simon after the man had moved away to try his luck at another bench. 'What a situation to be in! Poor bloody bastard! Don't you ever wish you could summon your magic for someone like that? Transport him overnight, like you do with us. I would if I were you.'

'Ah, but my powers,' replied Cody reflexively, 'do have most definite limits. You've a boss – Malcolm, right? – who tells you what you can and can't do. Well, it's the same for me...'

Then all at once he stopped. What did he think he was doing? He never spoke about such things. The whole point being: keep the machinery invisible. Make sure your charges concentrated on themselves, not on what happened behind the scenes.

'You have a boss?' Simon was intrigued. 'That never occurred to me! Puts a whole new spin on things. Makes you seem...'

'What?' demanded a nettled Cody.

Simon grinned. 'Less Olympian. More like one of us.'

'Really?'

'Really. And it's nice. It's relaxing. Although I still know too little. Like when we were talking yesterday, in that awesome square, which was also really nice, by the way, you said – remember? – how much you'd like to have a garden of your own. Yet do I know where you live? I guess it must be a flat, if you don't have a garden. But which city, if it is a city? And where did you grow up? Your parents: what of them? Just how did you get into this business of taking people around in the first place? What qualifications does a person need? In fact, how the hell does any of it work?'

At the same moment, he was remembering with a smile – and Cody was noticing, not for the first time, what an appealing smile the young man had; what pearl-like teeth – how natural it had seemed, while an accordion played, to be in Cody's company in that awesome square and for his eyes to then drift to that fountain where an octopus was coiled about the limbs of Neptune, less in battle than in a sinuous embrace.

'Thinking of squares,' he heard himself saying, 'I have this weird dream that's set in one. Except there I'm lost and the square is quite threatening actually and although there's always someone who might be able to help me, I can never make them out, I can't ever reach them. Then all at once the dream comes to an end, with me still lost, always lost.' He shivered. 'But why am I telling you this? Here of all places! When I'm so relaxed.'

A pair of green eyes looked long and hard into a pair of questioning brown ones.

'Perhaps it's *because* you're relaxed,' suggested Cody. 'For a change. I know this trip hasn't always been easy. And it's good. I wouldn't fight it.'

Whereas he himself, he was thinking – he needed to fight his own feelings with every weapon at his disposal. Unless he wanted to break all the rules in the fucking book! Getting involved with a client – what would Cedric have to say about that! He could just imagine and it wouldn't simply be a long and welcome break he was being offered; it'd be something altogether more final and much less welcome.

Although, by the same token, since it had been the opportune appearance of that beggar which had started this whole exchange of theirs, how was he to know that Cedric didn't already have a finger in this particular pie?

'But anyway, dreams,' he said aloud, dispelling the thought. 'Beyond my remit, I'm afraid. As I was explaining earlier, my powers do have limits. It's only by day that I have any sort of responsibility. And then only to a degree.' He rose decisively. 'But enough of all this dawdling! Come!'

On their way out of the park, they passed the formal gardens again, with their neatly trimmed hedges, geometrically arranged, and their careful lines of potted miniature trees.

'Okay, so I suppose,' said Simon, giving their layout one last look, 'that it does have its place, all this formality. And the actual process of gardening itself is, of course, just as absorbing either way. More so even, with the hedges. Placing them right. Can't be easy. Time probably slows even more.'

'Sorry?'

'So one of the things I like best,' explained Simon, 'about gardening, is how easily you can get lost in it. Time sort of slows down. Becomes sort of dreamy. Hours go by without noticing. Like in a trance. And I'm guessing the same would be as true or even truer here. It's the act of gardening that counts, more than the outcome.'

'The act,' echoed Cody. 'As in all things. Of course. It's always the act.'

***

The man Geoffrey had noticed at the window with the iron-grey hair and the teeth had long since vanished, to be replaced in an aural form by a set of earlier versions as Margaret told Geoffrey her full story; unexpurgated. She'd already covered that first week in Rome, or the bare bones of it anyway, but there was still stuff to add. Like the moment when Gustavo had finished painting her portrait, for example. How exposed it had made her feel, the sight of him casually setting down his brush and pushing his paints to one side. More than sitting for him ever had. She could still remember just how he'd turned her portrait to the wall because, he said, flesh was better – *realidad* was the word he used – and how shaky that had made her feel. How she'd started to cry and how he'd teased her for being so much, too much the weeping woman. *Mujer llorando.* Men preferred not to cry, he said. It was their job to stand firm. Like a rock. And that was how she'd clung to him too, as if caught in a riptide, and he was her only hope. Or, as she'd also thought at the time, like she was the cat – healthy, in her case – with the cream. Couldn't stop licking. Shameful, really. Until another cat – a sick one; his aunt's – had brought her up short momentarily.

But only momentarily. For with the next morning's extravagant bunch of flowers, she'd forgiven all – and so now she moved the story on to when she'd said goodbye to Gustavo as she and the others (the jealous others) had boarded the bus that would take them to Fiumicino Airport. That last adhesive embrace, that last wrenching wave and how she'd watched a Roman crowd swallow him up as he strode off along a thronged pavement. That tearful flight home and her mother worrying that she hadn't been taking sufficient care of herself, she looked so wan. But then her mother had always mistrusted foreigners and their cooking. Too fancy, she said. It didn't nourish; not properly; not like the Anglo-Saxon variety. Although Margaret's paleness (then and later) had nothing at all to do with the presumed shortcomings of Italian food. What ailed her was another kind of shortcoming altogether; the painful lack of a letter; the letter, letters even, he'd promised faithfully to write and never did.

The memories came in the form of punchy vignettes, much like the scenes from the period movie she'd run in her head the day before, and this too is how she related them to Geoffrey: kaleidoscopically.

She is walking past their old house on her way from the shops to the other side of the village, to where Susan and Henry now live and where she is also staying until she can sort herself out. It's been over a year without a letter. She hears her name being called. The woman who bought their old home is standing on the doorstep with something in her hand. Tentatively, Margaret approaches. The woman opens her mouth. 'For you,' she says, arm extended. 'Came the other day.' Margaret sees that the stamp is a foreign one, although at this distance she can't be sure of the country. Only when she's grasped the envelope does the stamp reveal its provenance: *Argentina*.

'That's better!' says the woman. 'You look so pretty when you smile. Sorry, I would ask you in, but it's a Thursday, the cleaner's here.'

'Not to worry,' gulps Margaret, barely able to restrain herself from ripping open the envelope on the spot. 'I'm in an awful hurry. As it happens.'

Like any major airport, Ministro Pistarini International, also known as Ezeiza, can overwhelm the uninitiated; and some months later, as Margaret emerges from the luggage hall into the arrivals area, it's as if she's been shoved onto a brightly lit stage. She blinks foolishly; feels scriptless; thanks her lucky stars that the other player has matinee idol looks and the unbounded confidence to go with them.

'Welcome to my city!' he says. 'Come, I take your bag. Let us go!' No fumbling of lines there.

Still blinking, she's in the doorway to Gustavo's first-floor apartment, he having dashed ahead of her into the bedroom to dump her suitcase. There's an easel by the window, presumably because the light is better on that side of the room. The painting on it is of a woman, although since the cubism of his style is now more pronounced, it's hard to be certain. One has to guess. She looks at the bookcase, full of books that aren't English; which you can tell, she finds, just by looking at their spines. The sofa is a doubled-over futon, covered by a colourful throw. And in the centre of the room stands a table with the remains of breakfast on it. A basket of bread. A coffee cup. Some jam. A sticky spoon. An over-flowing ashtray. Still-life elements of an existence she knows next to nothing about. Oh, she is mad to have come! And when she thinks of the circumstances involved, of Susan back home, it feels as though she might faint. She grabs hold of the door jamb in an effort to steady herself. What in heaven's name is she doing here?

'Why so shy?' asks Gustavo, emerging from the bedroom. 'Come in! Sit! Don't be slow! *Mi casa es tu casa*. You must know the saying?'

As Margaret came to the end of this, her third vignette, Geoffrey said: 'Well, well! Quite the heart-breaker, obviously! I can see why, if that really was him we passed on our way here, coming through the old city gate –' he didn't allude to the café window afterwards – 'I can see why his presence should have affected you so. Because don't imagine I didn't notice. It was impossible not to.'

She scowled. 'Bloody Cody! First the Doria Pamphilj Gallery, that was no accident either. Then today's little nudge just for good measure. Although as I said, it's ages since we saw each other, Gustavo and me, so I'm only guessing at how he actually looks these days. He might not have aged so well.' Her scowl became almost a smile.

'Indeedy!' allowed Geoffrey with a semi-smile of his own. 'Can sometimes happen.'

'Even to the most handsome of men.'

'Even then.'

'But in those early days,' she went on, 'there was never any question about his looks. You're right. He was a heart-breaker.'

It is a further few months later, Margaret has been back to Suffolk in the meantime, but is now in BA again, hopefully with a better sense of her lines, of what she must say to Gustavo in order to make things come right. She is standing at the window of his apartment. It is early evening and the street below is in shadow, which is why it takes her a while to be sure of what she is seeing there. Gustavo has gone out earlier to visit a painter friend, or so he says, but has promised to be back in time for them to go to the cinema together. He considers the dialogue of V/O films to be an excellent – also pleasant – way of helping Margaret with her Spanish. A language she will need if everything does pan out as she intends.

What she now sees, though, and the first-floor perspective from which she sees it, plus the shadowy, atmospheric lighting, throws the future into doubt while also making this vignette the most starkly cinematic of them all. V/O with a vengeance. There is even music on the soundtrack: a CD of Gustavo's, some tangos, that she's been playing to herself.

As backdrop, we have the lighted window of a shoe shop containing many examples of its merchandise, men's on the one side, women's on the other, some of them spot-lit, all of them stylish; the shop is high end. Swaying in time to the syncopated music, Margaret resolves to treat herself to a particular pair she's noticed more than once in walking past the shop – they are red, the shoes, and have buttons – although she will only do this after she has successfully had the conversation with Gustavo that she knows she can't put off any longer. This very evening ideally. Post-movie. They can talk then.

But now a woman steps into frame. Dark-haired, in a summery frock. She pauses to glance into the shop window, possibly at the red shoes, which would certainly match her dress, since that is red too, with a swirling pattern on it of yellowish leaves. Then she turns from the window and Margaret can see that her lipstick is as red as her attire. A man comes into frame also, where he surreptitiously clasps the woman by the hand, as if in coded farewell, and now all the camera sees is that his hair as it passes through the shot is honey-coloured.

Margaret steps sharply backwards. At the same time, she almost falls over the easel that still stands there, flaunting its cubistic representation of a woman. And what is the woman wearing? A red dress, of course, with swirling yellow patches on it, leaf-shaped. Red lipstick too. The final straw.

Though talking of straws, there does remain one to clutch at, even if she has to skip forward in time in order to do so. But this still feels necessary. Otherwise the story is too hard to tell. Too eviscerating.

She places herself at another window, the window of her own apartment, the one she finds after moving out of Gustavo's. A canvas that is so far mercifully blank. It is early morning and a bell is tolling from the solid church tower that rises like a rock above the dawn-tinged swell of the roofs. A different sort of rock entirely to the one represented by Gustavo. On this rock, you're not so likely to be dashed into a million pieces. Or if you are broken, it's only so that you can be made whole again. Can rise above yourself, just as the sun is rising above the many rooftops.

'And,' said Margaret in conclusion, rummaging once more for her crumpled tissue, 'there was the *Hogar de Caritas* too and the children I got to know there. Manuel, Gloria, Florencia, Joaquin. They also provided solace.'

'Well, I must say,' exclaimed Geoffrey, taking a last sip of coffee (it had got cold while Margaret was talking), 'he does sound, this Gustavo guy, kind of flakey. You're well shot of him, I'd suggest. And in fact, I don't altogether understand why he still bothers you so.'

'Because of Simon naturally.'

'Your nephew?'

'Don't you see? He's not my nephew at all.'

'He isn't?'

'Of course not. I'm his mother.'

'His mother!' Geoffrey's cup made a pinging noise as he set it down on its saucer. 'And his father...?'

'Who else!' replied Margaret, tissue held tight. 'Who else do you imagine it could be?'

Day 6

Because it was a Sunday, the sound that woke Geoffrey was one which had also featured in Margaret's tortured tale; that of a slowly tolling church bell. And to begin with, confusedly, he even thought that's where he might still be; in a café in Trastevere, caught up in an agitated woman's life story. Then he opened his eyes.

The curtains at his window were filmy and he could quite easily make out, by the filtered light, the room's principal features: fake antique furniture that had seen better days – there were scratches on the back of the nearest chair and what looked like burn marks on the side of the dressing table; there was a cobwebbed chandelier hanging directly above the bed; and, on the wall opposite, a dusty print in a ludicrously ornate frame, telling him all else that he needed to know. It was of a night sky, straddled by the unmistakable outline of a floodlit Eiffel Tower.

He went at once to the window, drew back the insubstantial curtains and there, in the distance, was another give-away: domed Sacré Coeur, source perhaps of the tolling bell. Though any excitement he felt in being, finally, at the head of the queue, so to speak, city-wise, was tempered by the fact that whatever came next, it was inevitably going to involve more of Margaret and Simon, since she'd yet to make her revelation to the man who up to now had thought of himself as just a nephew. So far only Geoffrey knew the full story. And what a story it had proved to be! He ran over it again in his mind.

How she'd met a young Argentinian in Rome. How they'd started an affair. How, after she'd returned home, the Argentinian had not, as promised, written, despite declarations of undying love. How, when she'd returned to her final year studies, she'd discovered she was pregnant. And still no letter from Gustavo.

Nor could she write herself because, by now, he might very well be back in Buenos Aires. He was only temporarily in Rome. So she'd abandoned her degree and slunk home, where she was rescued from having to explain herself in too much detail by her father's sudden and shocking desertion of the family, followed by her mother's cancer diagnosis.

Margaret had done her dutiful best to nurse her mother until, after a bare few months, the ambulance came to take her to a hospice. Meanwhile Susan, who'd recently married Henry, had herself become pregnant. Who'd have thought! Unless of course it was her surprising pregnancy, rather than a shared love of Christ, that had caused the hasty marriage? Margaret's thoughts on the subject were not particularly charitable.

Then came another shock. Susan's pregnancy was phantom. The only baby due was Margaret's. *And* she could no longer hide her bump, certainly not from a hyper-vigilant Susan, who now persuaded Margaret to move in with them and have her baby there. She also began her campaign to get Margaret to give Simon up. Not for out and out adoption; nothing as brutal as that. What Susan had in mind was much subtler. She proposed that she and Henry should take over because, being a couple, they could more properly care for a child. Surely Margaret could see the sense in that? Also, she'd then be free to finish her degree in Visual Arts and it wasn't as if she was going to be denied access. She'd just have to pretend to be the aunt. That was all.

At this stage of the story, Geoffrey, who could barely credit what he was hearing, had asked Margaret how she could have even borne the idea? For so much as a single minute. And indeed, it transpired that Margaret hadn't simply acquiesced to Susan. There'd been a string of contributory developments.

First, a letter from Gustavo. Back in Buenos Aires and thinking of her constantly. No mention of why he's not written before. Just – might she visit? Well, of course! But can she arrive carrying a baby? She doesn't think so. Nor does she think she can tell Gustavo about Simon in a letter. Or by email, because in his letter, Gustavo has given her a current email address. The phone is equally impossible, although she has also been put in possession of a number. So, in the end, she decides to leave Simon with Susan and Henry for a short while. Go alone to BA. Tell Gustavo face to face. Then introduce him to his son.

But when she gets to BA, although Gustavo seems delighted to see her, when she tries to raise the subject – which she does hypothetically, in the most general of terms, as in: how would you feel about becoming a father? Have you ever given the matter any thought? – she discovers that this is the last thing he would want. Can't she see he's an artist? Babies only get in the way. He's watched too many of his friends become similarly trapped. So, no! Not for him! But what he does want is Margaret. She's his muse, he says. Ever since their week in Rome, she's been in his thoughts. And although at first he tried to resist because it seemed impractical – the distance, language, different cultures – ultimately he just had to write to her. Couldn't stop himself.

So what does Margaret do? She returns home is what she does. To consider her options. Or rather, Susan considers them for her. It's been quite a success, her short stint as Simon's surrogate mother. The baby hasn't appeared to miss Margaret in the slightest. Such a contented little chappie! Then a doctor friend from the church comes by to back up what Susan is saying. Other arguments are trotted out: single mother versus married couple; the precarious versus the secure; stigma versus social acceptance. It's the good of the baby they should be concentrating upon, lectures Susan. And when you also take into account all the other pressures of that year – their father's sudden defection, their mother's sudden death, the emails Gustavo is now bombarding her with, pleading with his muse to come and live with him – the case can almost seem cut and dried.

She reaches a decision. She will return to Gustavo, leaving Susan in charge of her baby once more. But only briefly; only until she can find the right moment in which to tell the father about his son, whereupon he will surely recant and want her to go and fetch him.

But now is when she looks down on that shoe shop and sees a couple in front of it. Now is when she realises that while she's been away, Gustavo has found another muse. Or maybe the other muse was always there and Margaret was just a stand-in? She will never know.

While retelling Margaret's story to himself, using his own words when he couldn't remember hers, Geoffrey had been staring out of the window in the general direction of Sacré Coeur. But without registering much; Margaret was his principal point of focus. Then there came to him the sound again of a church bell and his eyes did consciously settle on the triple domes and he was hurried forward in the story to that moment when its heroine had also stood looking out over the rooftops, had also heard the sound of a church bell.

Geoffrey imagined her running down the stairs of her building, out into the Sunday streets. Did he know it was a Sunday? No, but in his version it was. Like today. He saw her running along a series of deserted pavements until she started to overtake a smattering of other people, all headed in the same direction. He saw her enter the church, find herself a pew towards the back, sink to her knees and he understood absolutely, one hundred per cent, why she should have felt as she had. After all she'd been through. Who wouldn't turn to a greater power in such a context?

Because after seeing Gustavo briefly touch the hand of the woman from the painting, Margaret had been stripped bare. She couldn't stay with Gustavo, that much was certain, even though he'd vehemently protested that the person he most truly loved was her. And to have returned alone to Suffolk, without any prospect of providing Simon with a father – how, up against what Susan and Henry could offer, was she to manage that? No! Better for the time being to stay put. On the far side of the world, where no one knew her. Where she could pass unnoticed. Might even – who knows! – find some slight redemption. Or, at the very least, limit the damage she'd already wreaked. Keep her head down. Stay still. Pray. Wait. Hope.

This was the point at which Susan drove her 'hard bargain', as Margaret had termed it. Said with a bleak little smile. Demanding of Margaret that, in return for giving Simon a stable home, Margaret was never to tell him she was his mother. Never ever. Under any circumstances. She must swear on the Bible.

Geoffrey turned from the window, thinking: then an accident involving a lorry allows Margaret to head home. If he'd been given the story to tell, would he have contrived the plot so? Or would it have seemed a trifle too convenient? And subsequently, would he have had her still feel unable to confide in Simon? Going so far even as to ensure that when he and Margaret returned from Trastevere to the hotel, Simon and Cody should be waiting there with yet more tickets, Simon having expressed a sudden desire to visit the Colosseum. Because then what happened, after the Colosseum and a wander through the centre of the city, was that it was time already for drinks. Followed by dinner in another small and noisy trattoria, where naturally nothing of any consequence could be divulged by Margaret, not in public, not in company. No wonder she'd appeared to withdraw into herself!

Geoffrey went into the bathroom. It'll be fascinating to see, he was thinking, how today pans out. On all sorts of levels, theirs and mine. Though when he ventured downstairs later, having shaved, showered and written more extensively in his journal than normal, for there was a lot to set down, to his surprise, no one else was in evidence. No Margaret, no Simon, no Cody.

The hotel's dining room had the same pretensions to grandeur as his room. Another chandelier; two, in fact; more in the way of antiquey furniture; fussy curtains and a fussy carpet. Although as with his room, the chandeliers were visibly cobwebbed. The furniture needed wax. The carpet was frayed. Nor was the breakfast up to much: the fruit salad was tinned and the scrambled eggs, which came in a dented container, silver plated but badly tarnished, had long since congealed. No muesli either. The croissants, however, looked fresh; and the coffee smelled good. So this was what he plumped for. A croissant and some coffee.

After another half an hour or so, during which he wrote up more of his journal, he was still alone at the table, wondering whether he should maybe ask at the desk about the others? Then, because this was after all *his* city of choice and he was most curious to see what it might have in store for him, he resolved to leave a note rather, saying that he'd gone for a stroll and could they please leave a similar message for him should they decide on doing likewise.

The day wasn't sunny – cloudy, in point of fact – but it was nicely warm and he found moreover that suffused light quite suited this city he'd waited so long to see. Their hotel was in a very straight, very wide boulevard that was flanked by imposing buildings of grey stone mostly, all with steeply pitched roofs that had as many windows in them as did the buildings' facades; windows that were, on inspection, more door than window, being tall and wide in every case and often surmounted by a pediment. The work of Haussmann, he guessed, having done his fair share of explanatory reading over the years. Who hadn't, when it came to Paris?

He wandered the entire length of the block they were on, then essayed another, then a third, taking due note of the shops and offices he passed, the wrought iron entrance to a metro station, the similarly ornamental design of the streetlights, the paucity of traffic, it being a Sunday.

A Sunday in Paris – he was actually in Paris! City of his dreams. Now a reality. Then he thought: why not follow the Hemingway trail as he'd outlined it for the others in Amsterdam, at the start of this little adventure? *Les Deux Magots. Café de Flore. Brasserie Lipp. La Closerie des Lilas.* The bar at the Ritz. Shakespeare and Company. All those sacred names. He looked at his watch. Just gone ten and he'd said in his note that he'd not be long. But would they mind if he behaved otherwise? It wasn't as if Margaret hadn't more than enough stuff of her own to be dealing with in the meantime. Perhaps that's why she and Simon weren't around even? She might finally be telling her son the overdue truth. Besides, throughout the trip he'd constantly felt that no matter what they each of them chose to do, Cody was forever at the back of things, orchestrating their every move. So if he wanted to go wandering for longer than he'd said he would, maybe – just maybe – he was only doing the expected.

***

Cody hadn't been at breakfast because, just as he was preparing to leave his room, Cedric had rung again.

'Bad timing?'

'Not at all.'

'I half thought you might be at breakfast.'

'On my way.'

'But you've a moment?'

'Of course.'

'Good.'

'All yours.'

Something in Cedric's tone, however, despite his apparent breeziness, had set Cody on edge. Or was it just his own guilt at work? The memory of being in that park with Simon. Potential unprofessionalism, and on a fairly grand scale.

'How was Rome? How was yesterday?' asked Cedric.

Unprofessionalism which Cody knew must be nipped in the bud. And would be, he promised himself.

'Yesterday?' he asked, keeping his voice level. 'Why yesterday especially?'

'Well, we did have that text exchange the day before, if you recall, and while things sounded okay then, I haven't heard beyond that.'

Which only put Cody on even higher alert, since Cedric didn't usually expect to be kept in the loop. On some trips the two of them didn't communicate at all. So why now suddenly?

Voice still level, he told Cedric that although he might wish things in Rome to have progressed a little further with Margaret, the direction of travel was not unpromising and all it now needed was one final nudge. (Or was he putting too positive a gloss on things? As yet he'd no idea what that final nudge should be.)

So then he said: 'And anyway, at this stage they really don't need my constant presence. It's probably even best if, from now on, I keep to the wings more. Hold back where I can.'

'Always much better,' agreed Cedric, 'when they start to take their own decisions. It is, after all, our principal aim. To empower them. Wouldn't you agree?'

'Of course I would.'

'And what about you?'

'Me?' Cody's voice was no longer quite as steady.

Cedric's, however, reedy though it also was, remained entirely so. 'Yes, you. Is everything okay in your quarter?'

'Why wouldn't it be?'

'Good! That's what I like to hear. Though I have also been thinking about the break we've decided you should take and I wanted you to know, ahead of us settling things in detail when we meet next week, that as far as I'm concerned, you can have absolutely as long as you like. Months even, if you want. So please – in the next few days, when you're considering all of this, as I know you're bound to, do please bear that in mind. You're not to feel even slightly obliged. Okay?' And then, when no immediate reply was forthcoming: 'Do you read me?'

'I read you,' said Cody. 'Loud and clear. Thank you, Cedric.'

'My pleasure.'

Cody had been by the door when the call had come in, about to open it and go downstairs, but now he went back to the desk by the window, where he stayed for the longest of whiles, mulling things over.

Not unnaturally, being in that park with Simon took centre stage. Although in keeping with his promise to stay professional, he did battle also to think through *all* of yesterday, questioning at every turn whether or not he might have done things differently. Because quite apart from anything else, it was clear to him (as already admitted) that their stay in Rome had ended on too inconclusive a note.

Had it been an out and out mistake perhaps to go with Simon to the park by the Villa Doria Pamphilj, not only on his own account, but in terms also of the wider picture? At the time he'd imagined that by leaving Margaret and Geoffrey to wander alone through Trastevere, where she could practise her whole story (whatever it was) beforehand, he was affording her the surest way of arriving at her final goal. But in no shape or form, least of all regarding himself, had things worked out as hoped. After a late lunch together and their visit at Simon's insistence to the Colosseum, they'd meandered through more of central Rome: the Spanish Steps, Keats's sad little house, the Trevi Fountain. Where the effect on Margaret, despite her having expressed a desire to reacquaint herself with some of these sights because she'd so liked them previously, had been a marked withdrawal. To the extent indeed that dinner, which they'd eaten at another small and quite noisy trattoria near the hotel, had been terribly uneasy, even with Geoffrey doing his best (as the person least affected by the evening's undercurrents) to keep the conversation flowing. Or precisely because of that perhaps? Since, in reality, Geoffrey's best left much to be desired. As when he'd quizzed Margaret on the *Hogar de Caritas* and her role there, which apparently she'd told him about in some detail on their morning walk, but which she'd obviously no wish to go on talking about.

Or when, in a clumsy attempt to alleviate her discomfort by drawing attention to discomforts of his own, he'd gabbled too extensively and indiscreetly about his ex-wife, who sounded (in Geoffrey's telling) like a monster. Although presumably Howard, the second husband, felt differently. On this point Geoffrey was strangely silent.

Simon had then improved things somewhat – about time too! – by saying to Margaret that ever since sitting in the Piazza Navona with Cody, which was when the idea had first taken hold, he'd been thinking more and more how it might after all make sense to go to university. And study plants. Get a degree, but in a subject that also had some practical value where he was concerned.

Margaret had of course applauded this surprise announcement. *And* she'd thanked Cody for being, as she suspected, instrumental in Simon's possible change of heart. But then she'd withdrawn into herself once more and Geoffrey's renewed attempt to come to the evening's rescue by keeping the focus on Cody hadn't helped either.

'Don't think,' he'd said, having put away the best part of a bottle of red wine, 'that I've not been watching, because I have, I've been watching intently, and still I can't see how it's done. Will I feel differently when we get to Paris tomorrow, which I assume is our next stop? Or isn't it? Care to elaborate, Mr Magician?'

Meaning that for the second time in one day, Cody had to make determined use of the eye trick – a more than usually prolonged stare – before summoning the bill so that they could all return to the hotel and sleep.

And now? Now tomorrow was upon them already, Paris was outside the window, and again he would need all of his skill if he wanted this trip to end successfully. His last in a while, it would seem, thank heavens! Though before he could step aside he did need to come up with that final nudge, which so far he hadn't, despite all his mulling.

Going downstairs, he discovered that the dining room, although not empty, was most certainly empty of his three charges. He looked at his watch and saw that he'd been up in his room far longer than intended; it was much later than his usual time for appearing. So! They must have gone exploring without him. Which, in line with what he'd said to Cedric about holding back, not to mention the need for continuing professionalism, especially with his beady boss looking over his shoulder, Cody didn't actually mind. In a way, he even welcomed it.

Although how then to administer that final nudge? With everyone absent. A nudge that would cross all the t's and dot all the i's.

It would, he reckoned, take quite a bit of figuring out.

***

Because it would bring him within spitting distance of three of his desired cafés, Geoffrey decided to begin his Hemingway trail from the Saint-Germain-des-Prés metro stop. Although as he was unfamiliar with the city, other than through reading about it, deciphering which line he wanted, then how best to connect with that line and which direction to follow once he was on the line, took some doing. But eventually he puzzled it out: line 4, direction Bagneux Lucie Aubrac. And by observing the behaviour of other travellers at the stop he started from, which was the one with the wrought iron entrance he'd passed not far from the hotel, he was quickly able to work out what buttons to push on the ticket machine. Which in any case offered English as one of its languages.

Since it was a Sunday, the train wasn't crowded; yet there were still enough people on it to keep him entertained as he embarked on a favourite game: guessing what country these people came from. In most cases, France it seemed. Unsurprisingly. Not that anyone wore a beret, or had a string of onions around their neck, or anything like that. There was just a certain style in common; a certain *je ne sais quoi*. To borrow an appropriate phrase. Until they came to Châtelet Les Halles, that is, where a number of clear-cut tourists got on, including some Chinese. How many brief hours did they still have, he wondered with a covert smile, before being whisked to Switzerland and beyond?

At Saint-Germain-des-Prés, the first thing he saw as he came above ground was the bell tower of a church. Tall, imposing and square, it was built of greyish stone, had a number of arched windows let into its sides and was topped by a steep spire of grey slate. Such as Margaret, had she been present, would undoubtedly have gravitated towards. But she wasn't and, for himself, he'd of course other fish to fry and now he noticed that directly opposite the church, on the other side of a small square, or *place*, stood the first of his wished-for destinations: *Les Deux Magots*.

The café was on a corner, wrapped around which were wide green awnings giving shade to the tables and chairs that spilled onto the pavement. In addition, there was more outside seating in the *place* itself, in a hedged area covered by another green awning that also had the café's name on it. Absorbing every detail, Geoffrey walked slowly past this outside area to where, on the corner itself, he could peer through revolving doors into an elegant, high-ceilinged room furnished with red leather banquettes and a great deal of dark polished wood. So this was where Hemingway had once held court! Physically, he was as close to his dream as he'd ever come. And diagonally across the street, he now saw on turning from the doors, stood *Brasserie Lipp*; and if he went just one block further, there, he knew, on the next corner, would be *Café de Flore*.

Walking on, he looked into the latter as well, then crossed the street and came back to gaze into *Brasserie Lipp*, before deciding that of the three, the one he'd most like to patronise was *Les Deux Magots*. Not the inside, however, handsome though that was; outside was better for continued people-watching. So he found himself a table, not difficult to do as it happened, and didn't have to battle either for the attentions of an aproned waiter, from whom he ordered a coffee and, because his breakfast had been so meagre, another croissant.

The outward picture Geoffrey presented after the waiter had served him his coffee and croissant and he was sipping the one while breaking off crumbly bits of the other and licking his fingers between bites was one of blithe contentment. A man living his dream, you might have thought, were you a passer-by with the time and inclination to notice him as he sat watching you. But what you wouldn't, couldn't have seen, no matter how hard you stared, was the sudden turmoil of Geoffrey's mind as the reality of being where he now was collided with all the years of wishing. Because wishing can, of course, thrive regardless of context or history or fact. Wishing is not achieving; wishing is just wishing. But when even the smallest part of a wish comes true – like being in Paris at a café you've spent so much of your adult life dreaming about – then all the component parts of that same wish come into focus as well. Sharply; unavoidably; unforgivingly.

In the past, Geoffrey had always told himself that he'd never written the books he wanted to write – and felt sure he had it in him to write – because he lacked the time. Or else it was demands at work. Or that Isobel, after some initial encouragement, had managed in so many ways to pull the rug from under his feet. But what if it was only fear that had held him back? Fear of what he would discover in the course of pursuing his dream. Fear of possible failure. What if, in the final analysis, he could only blame his own feebleness of self?

Then came another tart, unwelcome thought: was this perhaps why he so liked to imagine himself as Hemingway? A problematic character at best: the drinking; the misogyny; the arrogance. Was Hemingway less a means of pursuing his dream than of side-stepping it entirely? Of putting the acting out of something before the thing itself. Of substituting the inessential, however vivid, for what truly mattered, however prosaic. Thinking more about what it might mean to *be* a writer than you ever did about the actual writing itself. The simple act of putting pen to paper. (Except it wasn't that, of course: simple. Not by any stretch of the imagination. Yet all the same.)

This tart thought was not only unwelcome, it was painful too; the ultimate laugh at his own expense and not at all what he'd been hoping for on this Sunday morning. But once it had occurred to him, there was no turning back. Never again would he be able to use Paris as protection from reality.

Meanwhile the waiter, having noticed that Geoffrey had finished his coffee and croissant, came over to ask whether the gentleman cared for anything else?

Where to start? thought Geoffrey grimly. *How much time do you have in that smartly pressed apron of yours?*

Although all he said was: 'Another coffee, please.'

Which he then sipped very slowly as he started coming to terms with his new position.

What a day it was turning out to be!

His ruminations were interrupted by a black man without shoes and in the most tattered of clothes – oversized shorts, a torn T-shirt – who, hands outstretched, was passing between the tables. To general indifference, it has to be said. People either ignored him or curtly shook their heads, often without so much as looking up. Geoffrey, however, felt immediately in his pocket. Enough that his own dreams should lie in pieces at his feet. Why should anyone else – particularly someone whose needs were quite obviously more pressing; what were his in comparison! – be made to suffer? And since he'd had the foresight, while in Amsterdam, to draw some euros as they'd been walking through the Jordaan before lunch, he could, without difficulty, peel off a couple of notes and extend a helping hand.

The man darted forward, almost knocking into the neighbouring table as he did so, grasped the money, smiled his thanks, stepped backwards.

'Good luck,' said Geoffrey. 'I wish you well.'

'You are English?' Amazed, the man paused in his retreat.

'Is that so very unusual?'

'I go England,' said the man. 'I have cousin. Oxford. You know Oxford?'

Geoffrey nodded.

'Good city?' He sounded anxious.

'Most people love it,' confirmed Geoffrey, wanting to be reassuring. 'It's certainly very handsome.'

'And there is work?'

'I guess. If you look hard enough.' Geoffrey reached into his pocket for a second time. 'But England isn't cheap. Not these days anyway. You might need more than you already have. So here! Take this as well and the best of British luck to you!'

Again the man darted forward; again he smiled; again he drew back.

'Safe travels,' said Geoffrey.

Without trying any more tables, the man vanished around the corner, going towards *Café de Flore*. Fearing perhaps that if he did hang about, something might happen to deprive him of the unexpectedly large amount he'd just been given. For when luck comes your way, it's prudent not to tempt providence any further. Isn't it?

Or so Geoffrey was thinking as he stared after the man. That and much more besides. For he'd no doubt in his mind, absolutely none at all, that what had just taken place had been somehow stage-managed. And by Cody, of course, their omnipotent guide. Who else? Although the crucial point was: why? What had this little encounter been designed to prove exactly? And how should he, Geoffrey, now respond?

Then it came to him. Cody was merely giving him the simplest of nudges. That's what this was about. Cody reminding him that all he needed to do, if he wanted to write, was to let his curiosity roam. Observe. Listen. Forget about himself for once. Forget about wanting to *be* a writer (that old trap again) and think only of the story. Because there were stories aplenty, important stories, stories of great moment, just screaming to be told. Starting with a man on his way to Oxford.

He let out a brief laugh. Could it be this easy? Surely not! Yet here he was, on the Hemingway trail, thinking precisely that. How easy it suddenly all seemed. How within his grasp. Achievable. In a flash. Just like that. Magic almost.

Providing, of course, you kept your eyes on the goal. Didn't allow yourself to be distracted. Neither by fear, nor by anything else. Just care about the story. Keep focused on the story.

Geoffrey couldn't remember when last he'd felt such certainty. It was a heady sensation and, because he didn't want it ever to end, he ordered a third coffee from the aproned waiter, with a brandy to accompany it, and went on sitting at his table for a good while longer, spinning haphazard tales to himself about any number of passers-by. Until, looking at his watch, he saw that it was high time to move on. Which he decided he'd do on foot to start with, before going underground again, and so it was that, after walking along the Boulevard Saint Germain and turning left into the Rue Saint-Jacques in order to head towards

Notre Dame, which he'd glimpsed in the distance, so it was that, without particularly meaning to, since in his current state of mind it felt irrelevant, he came upon the Rue de la Bûcherie and another stop on the Hemingway trail: the bookshop with the unforgettable name: Shakespeare and Company.

The double doors in the centre of its quaint facade, recognisable from photographs, stood open, inviting him in. Though as he moved forward to enter the shop, his eye was then caught by the cover of a book in the crowded window. Two books, actually, both with his name on them. One was: *Sweet Tooth and Sugar: Cautionary Tales*. The other: *Margaret's Story*. The former being a collection of short stories; the latter a novel, or so it would appear. Each of them ostensibly his!

Gob-smacked, Geoffrey looked from one to the other and then back again as he drank in every detail of their cover designs. A jazzy arrangement of pink and purple triangles for the stories; the shadowy outline of a female head for the novel. There was also a shared strapline taken, it said, from *The Sunday Times*: 'A writer in total command of his material.'

Total Command! His material! The sort of plaudit any author on the planet might covet. And the other books in the window display bucked him up as well; the excellent company he was being permitted to keep. His mouth, which was by now hanging open, shaped itself into the broadest of smiles. So what if this had occurred without him even knowing? Because of course he could again guess who, and who alone, must lie behind it all. But he wasn't going to let any such consideration interfere with his full enjoyment of the moment and he hastened inside to where, in a room lined floor to ceiling with books, books absolutely everywhere, he almost fell over a table on which, among a handful of other choice titles, were copies of both *Sweet Tooth and Sugar* and *Margaret's Story*.

He snatched up the stories first. Apparently they'd been written over a number of years, starting when the author had been living in a basement flat in Stoke Newington. The very title indeed of the opening story: *A Basement Flat in Stoke Newington*. Then came: *Geography for Beginners*. Followed by: *Our Mutual Friend the Lodger*. So far so familiar; although after that the titles began to trace a life that Geoffrey wasn't so aware of; the life presumably of someone now published, who'd gone on to write an acclaimed novel – this he picked up too – about a woman who'd allowed her sister to lay claim to her only son.

Geoffrey paged through his latest creation, discovering phrase upon phrase which, although he was coming to them as if for the very first time, still felt known somehow. Then all at once he heard muttered voices, also known, a man's and a woman's, emanating from an alcove to his right. The woman sounded quite exercised and was saying in a fierce undertone: 'I know it's meant to be fiction, but who is he trying to fool? You've only to look at those early stories! Where I featured once, you may remember. You did too. He took his revenge on both of us. Art as a mirror to nature and all that high-faluting crap he used to spout. His way of getting at us, more like. And I refuse to believe it's any different with this Margaret creature. He's obviously found himself someone who's prepared to put up with his arrogance and what he now wants is to rub my nose in it. Just look at how soppily he writes when it comes to the scenes involving her. All that fake compassion. Huh! And don't pretend he doesn't! I'm not blind, Howard, I'm not a fool. I can see things for what they are.'

Barely trusting the evidence of his own ears, Geoffrey peered cautiously into the alcove and was thus able, because they both had their backs to him as they stood together over another small table, on which were more of his books – in this shop, his presence was inescapable; triumphant; like a flag on a mountain top – was thus able to watch unobserved as Howard, who'd grown a little stouter since the last time Geoffrey had seen him – *and* suffered some thinning of the hair – now pulled Isobel into an awkward embrace; awkward because the alcove was a narrow one, space at a premium.

'There, there!' murmured Howard. 'It's our anniversary, remember? We came away to celebrate. Not dwell on the past. You've given that bastard enough of your life already. Don't let him cast a shadow over the rest of it and all that we've fought to achieve.'

Again Geoffrey had to wonder at what he was hearing. *That bastard* – really? *Fought to achieve?* When, as he'd discovered around the time of the divorce, Howard and Isobel had first slept together when Howard was still their lodger, in the days when he imagined he still had Isobel's unstinting support and Howard was friend to them both. And although the lovers had then managed to restrain themselves – they'd only slept together the once apparently and Howard had remained, on the surface at least, a mutual friend – when things between Isobel and himself had hit their all-time low, who had been on hand to scoop her up? No! If there was a bastard involved, Geoffrey didn't feel it fair for Howard to be fingering him.

Thinking which, he found himself studying the bony fingers of Isobel's left hand as it snaked itself for reassurance around Howard's thick neck and he remembered how once he'd liked to take those fingers into his mouth and suck on them. She'd liked it too.

'I would remind you,' Howard was saying, still holding onto Isobel, 'how happy we both were until we walked in here. You love Paris. I love Paris. It's our city, darling, the first we ever ran to when living with Geoffrey became unbearable for you. All right, I do admit, it's unfortunate, coming across all these copies of his new book – I wish you hadn't read it before we left; I did warn you – but when we walk out of here, which is what we're going to do in a minute or two, Paris will still be Paris and we'll take every care to avoid further bookshops. Though I don't imagine, for all his fame, that he'll be in all of them. This is quite a special shop, I seem to remember.'

'True,' replied Isobel, somewhat mollified; a wistful note had crept into her voice. 'He used to talk about it all the time. Hemingway, remember? Always banging on about bloody old Hemingway in the early days.'

'Boy, could he bore the pants off one!' For his part, Howard sounded sorely resigned. 'I know he was once a good friend of mine, yet if I've learned anything in life, it's to beware of writers. I'm sure there must be exceptions – of course there are – but if what you do requires you to sacrifice everything in order to achieve it, then it shouldn't come as a surprise if that includes wives and old mates.' He pulled Isobel even closer. 'Let him have his art. It's thanks to his art and his commitment to his art that we get to have each other. And for that I shall always be grateful.'

So transfixed was Geoffrey by all of this that he'd begun unconsciously inching closer and now stood in danger of discovery should Isobel and Howard break off their embrace and turn around. He swiftly withdrew therefore; and just as well, because no sooner had he retreated to the other side of the alcove than Howard and Isobel emerged from it. She was leaning against her husband and it surprised Geoffrey to see her looking so vulnerable, so in need of protection. Not at all how he remembered her. But then his morning in Paris had been full of such salutary surprises.

Right now, however, he'd another matter to concentrate upon; and as soon as Isobel and Howard had disappeared back into 'their' Paris, he grabbed hold of some copies of his novel and of the stories, took them to a till, paid for them and then slipped his precious cargo into his trusty old leather bag, which hitherto had only ever been required for notebooks.

***

While Geoffrey was in the process of paying for his books, Margaret and Simon were walking from the Pompidou Centre towards Notre Dame, their morning having started with an early knock on Simon's door from Margaret in order to inform him that she was going in search of a church and would he please tell the others not to wait for her at breakfast? She'd grab a little something for herself afterwards. But when Simon had come to the door – his night had been more than usually dream-troubled and he was dressed already – Margaret had, with alacrity, grabbed the opportunity her son now presented.

'Come with me?' she asked. 'I don't have to go to church. We can just walk around for a bit, you and I. Wouldn't that be nice? Find ourselves a coffee somewhere, and a croissant. We're in the right city, after all, for croissants.'

'Plus, I've only ever seen the outskirts,' said Simon obligingly. 'Disneyland, not the same thing at all. Although I do remember, all the same, how awesomely excited everyone was. Fizzing, in fact.'

'I can well imagine.'

'Drove the poor teachers mad.'

'I wish I'd been around to witness it.'

'Really?' He stepped into the corridor. 'Right pains in the ass, I think we all were. A lucky escape, that's what I reckon you had, Auntie M.'

'Oh,' she replied quickly. 'I wouldn't say that. Anything but.'

They went outside, where it didn't take long for them to find a café they both liked and for Simon to add, once they'd finished ordering and before Margaret could begin speaking herself: 'Talking about being a pain in the ass...' But here he hesitated, a look of some doubt clouding his face, making his habitually mournful eyes seem sadder than ever.

'What?' demanded Margaret, thrown by this sudden development. 'What is it, dear? Spit it out! Please!'

'So!' said Simon, gathering himself. 'When I told you about myself on that lake in Switzerland and you were so good about it, and you really were, I should have known you would be. Sweet Auntie M, the best a boy could ever have! But anyway – I've noticed since, like in Rome, how tense you've seemed at times and...' Again he hesitated.

'Go on,' said Margaret quietly.

'So I just wanted to clear the air,' he said. 'Make sure there aren't any lingering doubts or misunderstandings. Because there have been things in our family, haven't there? – as with any family, I guess – that we don't really talk about and I suppose I'm saying that although most of these things are ancient history by now, I still feel it's best if we have everything in plain sight.'

And here it was, you might have thought: the perfect opening, the one she'd been aiming for, handed to her on a plate! But Simon was on an unanticipated roll. Besides which, as he continued to lay out his stall, her fear of doing likewise only intensified, making the task before her seem ever more Herculean. So, for the time being at least, she just went on listening.

He spoke first about Alison, reiterating how, if it hadn't been for her change of sexual direction, he might still be avoiding his own situation. He also made it clear that, as yet, he'd not told Alison all that he'd confessed to Margaret on the boat. Why? Because at that stage some doubt, some confusion still remained. Only in Switzerland had everything clicked into place. And for this he had Cody to thank as well. He'd needed a push from Cody. *And* Richard. The boyhood friend whom Margaret so mistrusted. He'd also needed to see him again in order to be absolutely sure and he now explained more fully about the encounter on the glacier. He talked about how Richard had made him feel over the years, the bullying and the teasing.

Then how, in the end – for light relief, this – Alison had broken up with him by text, saying: 'Richard may be dim, but he can at least read.' Which had made them both laugh.

He assured his rapt listener that even though he and Alison could never become an item themselves, this really didn't matter. She would always be central; would always feature; her ability to make Simon question things, the quality Margaret so admired, would not be lost.

Then he apologised all over again for his outburst on the train going up to Jungfraujoch, reaffirming his wish to go to university. To make something of his life. He said he understood that Margaret's fussing was entirely well-meant. What were aunts for, after all, when a boy had no mother? If not to chide!

(Another golden opportunity, not taken.)

And so he came finally to his relationship with his dead parents. How difficult it had sometimes been, largely because of the strictness of their views. Something rather cold in them that he couldn't wholly fathom. Sorry to be disloyal.

(Here again! Even more so!)

But then there was a lot he didn't understand, he said, when it came to family. Like why Margaret, a believer herself, albeit of a different order, should have been quite so happy to see him lose his own faith. Not that he was complaining, mind.

(And again!)

Or going back in time, to the ancient history, for him at least, why his father and his uncle, the one who'd gone to live in New Zealand, should have become estranged. Or why Margaret's father had walked out on them and what had then become of him?

By now they'd left the café and had, in passing, been admiring a great many fine buildings, pausing too to inspect a great many shop windows, all as Simon talked, until they'd come in sight of the north bank of the Seine. Specifically, the bridge that led to where the soaring cathedral of Notre Dame rose against the midday sky, also the point at which Margaret did at last find her voice.

She started with the easier stuff; well, relatively speaking. No one ever mentioned her father, she said, because after he'd walked out on them – just like that, there one day, gone the next – they'd none of them had the slightest idea what became of him. He'd simply vanished. And as for her brother-in-law, this was indeed ancient history, something she'd not witnessed herself and, because Henry never spoke about it either, she could only surmise. But she imagined it must have to do with Henry's conversion; with them not agreeing religiously. Since Henry's stern beliefs had underpinned most of what went on where he was concerned. She concurred with Simon there. A cold fish.

Taking care to add, in parenthesis, that he wasn't to think she was at all proud of how she herself had reacted to Simon losing his own faith. But there it was! In those days she'd welcomed any detachment Simon might feel from the memory of Susan and Henry.

And so it was upon her, the moment she'd been dreading and avoiding even while praying for its occurrence; although the voice she now heard as they stepped onto the Île de la Cité was not her own, but Geoffrey's.

'Margaret! There you both are! Over here! Look! Look at what the hell I'm holding! Can you believe it!'

He was standing some twenty feet away and, in his excitement, appeared much younger than normal. More of a satchelled, over-stimulated schoolboy than a teacher of schoolboys – like Simon maybe, on his visit to Disneyland Paris – and so, in accordance with this line of thought, as he began running towards the two of them, hand outstretched and a book in it, Margaret framed the moment thus: as if someone had fired a starting gun at a school race involving books rather than eggs and spoons, a race which Geoffrey was hell-bent on winning.

'Isn't it amazing!' The degree, however, to which he'd been robbed of breath by his short sprint made plain his actual age. He was panting like nobody's business. 'Ow! My ribs hurt!'

Smiling sympathetically, Margaret reached for the book that Geoffrey was thrusting toward her. A novel perhaps – then she saw the title and became aware at the same time of Simon shuffling closer so that he too could be privy to Geoffrey's excitement-inducing find.

She took great care not to move away before, very slowly, as if in a dream, she began to open the book, turning first to the blurb, which she proceeded to read, all the while ensuring that her hand kept steady so that the shadowy shape at her elbow could also devour its description of the novel's plot.

***

Having hit upon what he hoped would be an effective plan for Paris, Cody's next decision was that, after a solitary breakfast, he too should wander off; but with a special destination in mind.

Many years previously, when still a novice at the job, he'd been in Paris with a particularly tricky group. A couple on the verge of a divorce, who could barely stand to be in the same room. A film actor whose career was on the skids. A priest who feared he might be losing his faith. Plus a mother whose adolescent daughter, also in tow, had started cutting herself. It had taken all of Cody's budding skill to bring this lot face to face with themselves and their issues and in the early stages of the trip, which had started in Madrid, he'd more than once feared he was bound to fail. It had come as a distinct relief therefore when, upon their arrival in Paris, Cedric had suddenly appeared. And, in a matter of moments, by having the priest drag the adolescent to see the Mona Lisa and the film actor whisk the unhappy couple to a screening of the romantic comedy which had made his name, had set something in motion that, by the end of that week, would allow Cody to consider the job done. Cedric had also taken his protégé somewhere he would never forget: the *Musée Grévin*, on one of the city's grand boulevards.

It wasn't the wax figures that had made the impact. These, or similar, you could see in many such an establishment; Madame Tussauds in London, for example, to name perhaps the most famous. Providing you didn't mind queues. No, it was the initial hall of mirrors before you came to any figures, where the room changed its design even as you stood in the middle of it, that had impressed Cody most. All done with light and mirrors to make it seem as if the actual architecture was being re-shaped before your eyes.

'It's what they call a catoptric cistula,' Cedric had explained. 'The walls are lined with mirrors and you only need to alter one aspect for the entire room to appear different. Substitute a single tree, say, for a single pillar and when that pillar or tree is multiplied in the many mirrors, a room suddenly becomes a forest, inside becomes outside, or vice versa. Clever, huh?'

'So what are telling me?' Cody had asked. 'That it's easy?'

'Of course not! But we want it to *seem* easy. That's the magic. Making stuff happen seamlessly. In an instant. It must feel inevitable.'

Emerging now from the hall of mirrors, where once again he'd watched one kind of room change, within seconds, into another, going through the hall's whole cycle of possibilities, Cody walked quickly past the rest of the museum, not bothering to register who had been added or subtracted to the total of noteworthy figures since his last visit. He'd probably not even know who some of the recent acquisitions were – you had to keep bang up to date with every sphere of human activity in order to do that – and anyway, the hall of mirrors had once again, by virtue of its sublime ephemerality, elbowed all else aside and he stepped out onto the grand boulevard again much comforted by the thought that change is always possible; quite extreme change, if need be; and in an instant too; seamlessly; well, sometimes. Although it was as true to say that after the magic must come the mundane. The end of every trip also always meant a return to broad daylight and reality.

With all of this in mind – together with Cedric's exhortation over the phone that he should be considering his options – he began going in the general direction of the Seine, putting some leading questions to himself as he went. Like:

How long – since it was up to him to decide apparently – did he actually want his upcoming break to last?

Would he maybe like to do some travelling in the course of it?

On his own, though, how would this make him feel after all these years? Less or more lonely than he already did?

Although as this was also quite painful to think about, he immediately shied away from the question, asking instead:

How, in more general terms, did he see his future beyond the upcoming break? More of the same? Or something quite different?

For example: travel. Was a job that entailed so much of it still acceptable in an age where – increasingly – travel was becoming a no-no?

Or in an era when the world's problems were so acute generally – he wasn't just thinking about climate change here – by doing what he did, was he in effect merely applying a sticking plaster to a gaping wound?

Would his skills be better employed in some other sphere perhaps? For example, by tackling problems that weren't always so purely personal. Or did everything inescapably lead back to the personal? Many believed so.

In short: how did he, Cody, want to live his life from here on? When the room changed, how exactly did he want the room to look? Pillar or tree? Or something quite other? And was there ever to be a second soul in the room alongside him? Or would his journey continue to be a solitary one?

He was crossing the Rue de Rivoli as he posed this final question and here too was where he encountered the African asylum seeker in the oversized shorts and torn T-shirt, coming towards him from the direction of the Île de la Cité. It was a strange moment. The man had been holding out cupped hands to almost everyone he passed; on approaching Cody, however, he suddenly withdrew his hands and lowered his head, as if fearful of what might happen should he risk begging from the figure in white. Cody stepped sideways as a result and a sort of fumbled tango ensued as they danced around each other. Then the other was gone and Cody was left wishing that he did have it in his power to ensure the man a secure future. But, as he'd already let slip to Simon, his skills weren't infinite; and anyway, if anyone had control of the escapee from Africa, it was presumably Cedric. Playing at what, though? Since it was the man's unexpected appearance in that Roman park which had caused him to say what he had to Simon in the first place, about having a boss, which in turn had precipitated their most naked exchange of the whole trip.

Remembering all of which, he came at last to the spot before Notre Dame where Simon was looking at the book which Margaret held open in her hands, while Geoffrey stood to one side, looking proudly on.

Pausing in his approach, Cody watched intently as Simon took the book from Margaret and started to flick through its pages, brown eyes wide.

So! It had all come to pass then! Just as he'd hoped it would. Not bad for a morning's work. And with luck, whatever came next – because here his planning stopped; from this point on it was up to them – would successfully conclude what had been initiated. Although for the moment, Simon simply read on. Margaret didn't move a muscle. Geoffrey too stayed stationary.

Until eventually, having skimmed the entire book, Simon closed it, passed it to Geoffrey and, taking Margaret into his arms, gave his mother a fierce, protracted hug.

Cody resumed his approach.

'I wondered where I might find you!' he said on reaching the trio. 'Had a good morning?'

Geoffrey snorted with laughter. 'As if you don't already know!'

Meanwhile Margaret, who'd tears in her eyes, but was smiling nonetheless, laid a brief hand on Cody's arm and said: 'Thank you!' She turned to Geoffrey. 'And you! I'm not sure I could have done it otherwise. I was that scared. That terrified.' She looked at Simon. 'Of little old you! Imagine!'

'Mum,' said Simon softly, testing the word on his tongue. 'You're actually my mum. Not an aunt at all. Sainted or otherwise.'

'I do realise,' said Margaret, 'that there's a lot to explain still. An awful lot to digest. Geoffrey's novel can only be a beginning. And I'll do my best. Promise! But right now...'

'Right now what, Mum?' asked Simon. Then he giggled. 'No more Auntie M! How about that!'

'You can still call me Auntie M if you want.'

'No I can't. I can only call you Mum.' Again he giggled. 'Mum's the word. The only word.'

'My darling boy.'

'I rather think,' said Geoffrey *sotto voce* to their watchful guide, 'that you and I should make ourselves scarce. Wouldn't you say?'

Cody nodded. 'Couldn't agree more. Although first, what about another photo?' He took out his phone. 'Right, everyone! Stand together, please. United front!' He dropped to his knees so that he could get more of Notre Dame into the background. 'All smile!'

He took a couple just to be on the safe side and then, as the three of them disbanded, went to stand alongside Geoffrey, who said, still *sotto voce*: 'Shall we find ourselves somewhere for lunch perhaps? And while Margaret explains herself to Simon, you can do the same to me!'

Margaret, who'd slipped her arm into Simon's, said: 'Okay if we meet back at the hotel this evening maybe? Or late afternoon?'

'Of course,' concurred Cody. 'No hurry. You take your time.'

So Margaret and Simon went one way, while Cody and Geoffrey went another, into the Latin Quarter, where they soon came across a promising bistro, there being bistros aplenty on the left bank. And here, once they'd been served by the patron himself – the bistro was small and family run; an increasing rarity in twenty-first-century Paris, as Cody took care to point out – Geoffrey told their guide all about his morning on the Hemingway trail. The many surprises. The sharp lessons learned. Both about writing and, as it happens, his marriage. Being made to see unexpected Isobel afresh, through new eyes. Howard too, come to that.

'All very instructive,' he said. 'A whole new take on things. Like an alternate reality, sort of. Although I guess, of course, that much – if not all – of this you already know. But have you seen these? Properly, I mean.' And from his shoulder bag, he produced his two titles, holding them aloft with a flourish so that Cody could admire both cover designs. 'Quite amazing!' he grinned. 'Truly magical. *And* I've been able to use the novel to help Margaret too.' He patted it fondly. 'That's the real cherry on top.'

Then he returned his treasure to his bag, took a last mouthful of his meal, put his knife and fork together, pushed aside his plate, wiped his lips and said challengingly: 'So, Mr Magician! Please explain how it's done. You make everything look so easy, but I need you to pull back the curtain if you can – like in *The*

Wizard of Oz – and show us who's at those controls. Even at the risk of disappointment.'

'You're asking me to spoil the magic?' A smile had come to Cody's lips. 'That's the writer in you speaking! Wanting at all costs to get at the truth. The elusive truth.'

'I guess.' Geoffrey didn't contest the description.

'And if I said that actually it *is* all very easy, remarkably easy? That the answer lies within. That if there is a curtain, it's always an internal one and the person behind it is always yourself.'

'That easy, huh?'

'That easy.'

'And you're not saying more?'

'I can't. But what I can do is show you a little something, if you like. One of my special places. We've got all afternoon.'

'Show me what?'

'You'll see when we get there.'

They ordered a coffee and a cognac to finish and then, after calling for the bill, Cody suggested that they walk rather than take the metro to where he had in mind.

'This morning's cloud cover seems to have dispersed,' he said, pointing through the window. 'Looks like a lovely afternoon and we don't have to be back at the hotel until much later. Also, since it sounds to me like you've found what you need to find here, this might be our last day in Paris, we should make the most of it.'

As they walked, Geoffrey said thoughtfully: 'About magic, about truth...'

'What about them?'

'So I'm a great believer in synchronicity. I often think of someone, then walk around the corner and hey presto! There they damn well are. So I guess that actually, when you come down to it, there's a degree of magic in almost everything we do. What Margaret would call faith.'

The Paris sunshine was making them feel expansive and so, as they strolled on, *flâneurs* both, they discussed many such aspects of human existence, while also commenting from time to time on their surroundings, even some of the people they passed and whether or not, as Geoffrey had felt on the metro that morning, you could spot a French person (or a Parisian, more specifically) just in terms of outward show.

'Still far to go?' asked Geoffrey eventually.

'No,' said Cody. 'In fact, we're here. Look!'

He indicated the *Musée Grévin*.

'A wax museum?' Geoffrey sounded disbelieving.

'*I* was wanting to know more once,' said Cody. 'Still am, in many respects. These things never stop. But anyway, to give me a helping hand someone more in the know than I ever will be took the time and the trouble to show me this place. And I often come back, if only to remind myself.'

'Of what?'

'How one sort of space can sometimes change into another. Just like that. In a flash. Come, I'll show you!'

***

Much as Cody had expected, the hall of mirrors worked its magic on Geoffrey too – and once they'd left the museum to go in search of somewhere suitable for tea, he began to talk about himself in a way that Cody hadn't heard before. With a sort of rueful frankness that was quite disarming as he looked back over his marriage and the woman who, in the bookshop earlier, had appeared to him as other than her normal self.

He detailed their early days together in their basement flat in Stoke Newington, mentioning how beautiful she'd been, how sharp and observant, how funny. His better in so many ways. He'd fallen in love with her for good reason, he said tenderly, and it had been madness to let her slip through his fingers like he had. But the awful truth was, which he saw now: he'd been too wrapped up in himself and his thwarted desire to be a writer. Nor had it helped to be so dissatisfied with his job, which he did without passion really, simply to pay the bills. With the result that passion had leaked from him everywhere and he'd ended up not giving anything, not his writing, not anything, even a fraction of the time or commitment it needed. Instead, he'd taken to dreaming, which of course got him nowhere. In a nutshell, he was failing both himself *and* Isobel and although – despite a snatched night with Howard, as he'd later discovered – she'd stayed with him, it was at some personal cost. Clearly. Notwithstanding his nature, rather than because of it. And no wonder then that she'd become so shrewish. So critical. So sniping. His nemesis, just as Rome had been Margaret's. She who at the start of things had been purely supportive and now he told Cody about the beautiful pen she'd once given him. Brass, with a steel-coloured nib, which he'd used more as a prop for his Hemingway fantasies than to write with. Inadequate fool that he was!

All this was suddenly visible; plain as a Parisian day. Where before he'd only ever glimpsed the truth; in bursts at most, quickly forgotten. And he also now understood why Isobel should have turned, as she had, to Howard; patient Howard; in-the-wings Howard. He permitted himself a hollow, mirthless laugh.

'Quite a day it's been,' he said, 'for yours truly. Isobel and Howard and then my books, of course, which were an even greater shock. Thrilling, I won't deny how thrilling that was. But still a shock and it's going to take me quite some time, I fear, to work out where I go from here. But work it out I shall. What else are sabbaticals for? And anyway, I simply can't go on in the state I'm in. So!' He stared deep into Cody's dancing eyes. 'Like Margaret, I owe you a whole avalanche of thanks.'

Cody held up a deprecating hand. 'Just doing my job.'

'All the same, however it works – and it's okay, I get the message – it's much appreciated. Really it is. But now,' he continued, finishing his tea, for they'd been having this conversation on the terrace of a café not far from their hotel, 'I guess we should be heading back, join forces with the others. I wonder what the rest of *their* day's been like? Every bit the equal of mine, I hope.'

As they'd each of them already registered, for it was impossible not to, their hotel was anything but smart. Distinctly three star, in fact. But just off the lobby there was nonetheless a most pleasant and cosy little bar, which was where Cody and Geoffrey found the other two, ensconced in a corner, enjoying a martini.

'May we join you?' asked Geoffrey.

'But of course,' said Margaret. 'Please do!'

Further drinks were ordered – martinis all round – and while a diligent waiter from behind the bar prepared them, they discussed Paris. What a handsome city it was. How agreeable to visit. Why didn't they come more often? Or at all in some cases. Under three hours from London by train. What could be easier?

'Is it only the existence of the channel?' mused Geoffrey. 'Mere water. Or is something else at work?'

'Not bloody Brexit again!' groaned Cody, darting a look at Simon in order to assess whether the latter was at all tempted, as he usually was when the subject arose, to join the fray. Then, as quickly, he looked away again. Not wise, under the circumstances, he didn't think, to let his gaze linger.

'Does the simple fact of being an island,' continued Geoffrey remorselessly, 'inevitably mean you set yourself apart?'

'Aha!' cried Margaret, pouncing. 'But no man is an island. Ask not for whom the bell tolls and so on and so forth. It tolls for thee.' As a practising Catholic, she knew her Donne better than most.

'And so we come again to old man Hemingway!' grinned Geoffrey. '*For Whom the Bell Tolls*. Great title. He was good at titles, was old Papa.'

'Stop!' said Simon. 'All these literary allusions. You're making my head spin. I'm just a humble gardener, remember.'

'Although you have promised,' Margaret reminded him, 'you said it again earlier, that when we get back...'

And so the talk turned to how Margaret and Simon had been negotiating the day's disclosures since walking away from Notre Dame together, arm in arm. They'd sifted through pretty much everything, it transpired, starting with Margaret's relationship to her parents, the story of her grandparents before that, then Susan and how that relationship had developed, her trip to Rome and meeting Gustavo and the hard bargain that Susan had driven, Susan and Henry both. Although now that Margaret had told Simon the truth, she didn't want to lay too much of the blame at Susan and Henry's door. Or at Gustavo's, for that matter. Better, she felt, to acknowledge – and acknowledge fully – her own complicity in all of this. Her own selfishness. Foolishness. Heartlessness even. Now that Simon had hold of the story and could absolve her. Which, on the surface of things, he seemed most inclined to do, because when he in turn spoke about Susan and Henry, it became increasingly evident how ultimately unsympathetic they'd been as parents. Although differently to Margaret, he'd suffered at their hands too and on that score alone, if no other, he wanted Margaret for his mum, as he was now calling her. A mum who, when things had got really bad at home one time, had treated him to a skiing trip.

'Yes, well,' she said. 'I remember noticing a change of tone in your letters – and you were always so good about writing...'

'I was made to. A two-line whip.'

'Are you saying it was a chore?'

'Of course not.'

'Because for me your letters were an absolute lifeline and when I sensed from them that things weren't easy at home, I thought the least I could do was try and ameliorate matters. A skiing trip isn't much, but it's better than nothing.'

In this fashion, with reminiscence following reminiscence, they shared their happiness and amazement with the others, holding nothing back. Or so it seemed. Although Geoffrey did notice (Cody too) that very little was said about Gustavo. And when the subject of Rome came up, Margaret, who'd been carefully listing some of the old haunts she'd not visited in Trastevere with Geoffrey, but wished she had, if only there'd been the time, made no mention, none at all, of the man most responsible for making that first week of hers in Rome so memorable. The man who, as Geoffrey alone knew, had also, after walking through the old city gate of Porta Portese, later pressed his face to the window of that café.

No sooner had this thought occurred to him, however, than his and everyone else's attention was caught by the couple who'd appeared in the doorway to the bar and were standing there open-mouthed.

'What the fuck! Geoffrey! It can't be!'

The voice belonged to bony Isobel, although from the expression on the face of the man whose arm she was clutching, it could just as well have been his. Both looked astounded.

Geoffrey rose. 'Isobel!' he cried. 'Howard! Heavens!'

The pair, one stout, one not, began advancing across the bar.

'And this morning as well,' exclaimed Isobel, upon arriving at the corner table where the others were seated. 'Guess what we saw in this funny old bookshop we stumbled across? Piles and piles of your new novel. Like everywhere! Just can't escape you, it seems.' Her gaze expanded to encompass everyone. 'Sorry. Don't mean to interrupt.'

There was an awkward pause, broken by Geoffrey, who said: 'My congratulations, by the way. Because it is your anniversary, no? I do hope you're both having a splendid time?'

'Actually, we are,' said Howard. 'Thanks for asking. Paris has always been good to us. A special place. Hey, darling?'

'But now *I* need to offer my congratulations,' interjected Isobel. 'Your new novel – it's fantastic what you've achieved – and although this isn't easy for me to admit...'

'Darling!' Howard sounded worried.

'But if we'd still been together, I do ask myself whether it would have happened. I didn't always show you the necessary support, I don't think. Too jealous maybe. I hope you can forgive me?'

Her saying this – something Geoffrey would not have considered possible before –gave him a much needed boost of confidence. He'd yet to decide what exactly he was going to do once his sabbatical had ended, but more and more he was beginning to have some inkling.

'Though you did give me a pen once,' he said, 'which I still have and which I shall always treasure.'

'Ah!' Isobel's eyes dimmed. 'That pen. Yes, I remember that pen. Very fancy and if I'm honest, I gave it to you not just as an encouragement. There was a sneaky bit of me that thought it might also intimidate.' She let out a harsh laugh. 'We weren't always very nice to each other, were we, Geoffrey? You and I.'

Howard, who looked as though he wanted the floor to swallow him up, coughed embarrassedly.

'No,' said Geoffrey. 'I don't suppose we were. Faults on both sides.'

Isobel turned to Margaret. 'But I can see,' she added, smiling sweetly, 'clear as day that now it's different, all very different. And I've found happiness too, great happiness, with Howard. Haven't we, darling?' She pulled the embarrassed Howard close. 'All's well that ends well. Can we say that, do you think? Or is it too Shakespearean for words?'

There was another pause, this one stunned in nature rather than merely awkward, during the course of which Geoffrey could feel everyone's eyes upon him, including Margaret's. He didn't dare look anywhere but at Isobel.

'Don't hate me,' she said, still smiling. 'I know I'm a terrible person. But for once I mean well. Honestly I do.' She turned towards Howard. 'Come, darling,' she concluded. 'After traipsing about all day, I really do need a hot bath and the table's booked for when? Eight, did you say? Takes me longer and longer these days to put the war paint on.'

'Good to see you, old man,' mumbled Howard, adding for the benefit of the table at large: 'Sorry again for intruding. Have a good evening.' Firmly, he steered Isobel back into the lobby.

Geoffrey, who'd been standing all this while, sat down again, still without daring to catch Margaret's eye. Or Simon's.

Cody it was who ended the silence. 'Talking of dinner,' he said in his best tour guide tone, 'I know a place not far from here where the food's really good and as I'm sure we'd all like to freshen up too before we eat, why don't we meet back here at about eight thirty? Once the coast is clear. Okay?'

No one demurred.

Day 7

After their successful Sunday in Paris, which they'd rounded off with a highly convivial (also delicious) meal, Cody considered the job to be effectively finished with and so, in deference to Cedric's signature urge, recently reaffirmed, to bracket any trip with a degree of symmetry – a means, Cedric always maintained, of compensating for the many unknowns along the way – it had to be Amsterdam next, where he awoke on the Monday to the same unexceptional room as at the start of their trip. The generic built-in cupboard; the flat-screen television on the wall opposite the bed; the desk unit and mini-bar; the kettle and minimal means of making tea or coffee.

One last day they'd have in which to tie up any loose ends – there were always a few of those – and then, if it's Tuesday, why: they'd be home again, facing up to the rest of their lives.

Slipping out from under the duvet, he went to the window, where he saw, on drawing back the curtains, that the day was a grey one, wet with it. The canal-side cobbles were glistening. Not a day then for wandering around outside; they'd have to remain indoors as far as possible. No problem with that, however, in Amsterdam. Much to see in Holland's principal city; much to do. He'd make some suggestions over breakfast.

Except that when he did go downstairs a little later, the lift doors slid open at lobby level to reveal the sight of Simon's coated back as the latter sped for some reason out through the hotel's revolving door and into the rain. Then came another arresting sight: that of Margaret emerging from the dining room, looking frantically about her.

Cody went at once to her side.

'Is everything all right?' he asked.

'Have you seen him?' Close up, her cheeks were unmistakably tear-stained.

'Simon, you mean?'

'Of course I mean Simon. Who else would I mean?'

'Well, yes, since you ask, I did catch a glimpse just now, of him dashing out.'

'He's gone outside? In this weather! But he can't have!'

'No mistaking the shape of that head. Sorry!'

'Oh, dear!' Margaret looked more distressed than ever. 'What should I do?'

'Perhaps,' suggested Cody, 'you could start by explaining what this is all about. In the dining room, ideally, over coffee – I could do with a cup – where we can also sit.' He took her by the arm. 'Come!'

In the dining room, Margaret indicated for him to aim them towards a table in the corner that still had her bag on it and her phone and the remains of two breakfasts. Once there, Cody waved for a waitress, who, when she came, turned out to be the very one who'd served them at the start of their trip. Not that the recognition was mutual. But then why would she recognise them, thought Cody, with so many people coming and going all the time? It wasn't as if they were out of the ordinary, unless you counted Margaret looking upset. And even then – was a tearful woman that unusual? Distress of one sort or another was probably quite commonplace in this room.

'Right!' he said, after the waitress had served them their coffee. 'Shoot! Yesterday everything seemed pretty much sorted, I thought. You both looked content. So it puzzles me rather, truly it does, to see you in such a state.'

'I know,' said Margaret, taking up her cup. 'It surprises me too. All very odd. As if there's some sort of gremlin at work.' She put down her cup. 'But no! I mustn't fool myself. There's only me to blame.'

'In what way exactly?'

'I'm not sure how to start explaining.'

'I guess you were busy having breakfast together, the two of you – is that not as good a place as any?'

She made no immediate reply, however, reaching instead for the handle of her bag, which she began toying with; until Cody, losing patience, laid a restraining hand on her fretful one and said sternly: 'Margaret! The suspense is killing me.'

With an apologetic smile, she began detailing how she'd come down early because, being back in Amsterdam, she'd thought it might be nice to revisit the church she'd found on their last visit. But on going into the dining room for a quick coffee beforehand, she'd chanced upon Simon – 'sitting at this table, looking not himself' – which had of course caused her to ask him why he should be so glum. Whereupon he'd admitted to a sleepless night and, bit by bit, it had come out that he'd been obsessing (among other things) about Gustavo. Picking up on something she'd said the night before, during their dinner in Paris, when she'd happened to mention, with regard to him going to university, how much she'd always regretted not finishing her own studies, he suddenly said: 'So, Mum, if you really did want to finish them, has it never occurred to you that if you'd told him, instead of just walking away, it might actually have made that possible?'

'Why on earth would you think that?'

'Just that maybe, if you had confronted him, maybe you might also have reached some sort of eventual accommodation. I mean, it's not beyond imagining. You might even have been able to renegotiate things back home and I might have met him in due course, my dad, my real dad. It's none of it impossible.'

'You really think so?'

'I wouldn't say it otherwise!'

'And are you also saying that in fact this is what you really want? To meet up with him. Is that what this is all about?'

'So are you still in touch with him then?'

'Heavens, no!'

'But if you were...'

'What?'

'Would you mind if I did want to see him?'

And this was more or less how, said Margaret, their early morning conversation had unfolded.

'And of course I wouldn't mind,' she continued, having regained some of her equilibrium. 'It wouldn't be my place to mind. Though I did warn him that he shouldn't expect too much of Gustavo and I'm afraid my saying that seemed to upset him even more and certain other things were then said about the unreliability of parents in general that...' She grimaced. 'Things that would have been better left unsaid. And because I got a little upset afterwards myself, that's when he stormed out, poor lamb, leaving me here.'

'How awful,' murmured Cody. 'I'm so sorry, Margaret.'

'It's not your fault.'

And indeed it wasn't. All he'd planned for was some gentle indoor sightseeing. But it was still incumbent upon him to alleviate the situation if he could. How, though? Because as far as he could see, the most evident solution also carried the greatest risk. The thought of which made him keener than ever for the trip to be over. High time, he thought grimly, to go on his promised break and forget about other people and other people's troubles for a while. Think only of himself for a change.

'I know it's not directly me,' he went on, reaching once more for Margaret's hand, which he cupped in his. 'But I do still feel responsible. These trips I run, they throw up many challenges and you can get some nasty bumps along the way. But believe me when I say: this too will pass.'

'Sure of that, are you?'

'You've told him something that would be hard for anyone to digest, just as he's told you things about himself that weren't so easy either. He's still processing all this stuff. No surprise there.'

'I suppose you're right.'

Then he heard himself saying: 'And if you like...'

'What?' Margaret looked up from where her older hand was resting within his younger one. 'You have a new trick up your sleeve?'

'No trick,' said Cody, his voice sounding strange even to his own ears. 'Only that if you like, I can always go in search of him myself.'

'You'd do that?'

'If you'd like. But when I find him, if I find him, what then do I say? What do you want him to know, Margaret, most of all? I'd like for you to tell me precisely so that I can be sure of doing this right.'

'What I want him to know,' said Margaret slowly, giving due emphasis to her every word, 'is that yes, I am unreliable, extremely so. But that doesn't for one second mean I don't love him dearly. In fact, it breaks my heart after the last few days to think that we might be even in the slightest bit estranged. He's my son. I'm his mother. End of story.'

'Okay!' said Cody, rising. 'I will find him and I will tell him just that. End of story.'

Leaving Margaret to what remained of her coffee, he re-entered the lobby, only to discover that Geoffrey was by the front desk, asking something of one of the two young women on duty behind it.

Going straight up to him, Cody gave voice to a brisk: 'Good morning!'

Geoffrey swung round. 'Morning!' He looked startled; even a little guilty. 'So you're up too! And the other two? I was thinking I might be the first for once and I was just asking this lovely young lady here if she could let me have a map. Although I suppose that when it comes to mapping out our day, you're well ahead of us as usual. And in fact, apropos that, there's something I need...'

'No, no concrete plans as yet,' said Cody, cutting him short. 'There's not been time. Besides, Simon's gone AWOL and I've said I'll go looking for him. Margaret you'll find in the dining room.'

'AWOL? Is anything wrong?'

'He's a little upset, it would appear. Margaret can tell you more.'

'So – in that case, what? Just wait here for you? Is that what you'd like us to do?'

'Or go wandering, do, if you feel we're taking too much time. No problem with that. But leave word at the desk. We'll find you wherever.'

Thus instructed, Geoffrey disappeared into the dining room, while Cody continued towards the revolving door, where he was brought up short by the fact that it really did look wet outside. Not heavy rain, but the sort of persistent drizzle that could nevertheless drench a person. He'd need to go back to his room for a coat or his umbrella. He didn't even have his cap with him. Then he noticed that still hanging on the coat-stand by the door was the dark blue raincoat that Simon had seen as well, even fingered, during their last stay in the hotel. Moreover, it was the only garment on the stand and it hung there in a most inviting, not to say challenging fashion.

Take me! it seemed to be saying. *Use me!*

Cody glanced about him. The lobby was momentarily empty; the two women behind the desk, intent on their computers, both had their heads down; and if, as seemed likely, the raincoat had been hanging there unclaimed for a whole week, it quite possibly qualified as lost property. In other words, his for the taking! So take it he did and found, just as soon as he'd donned the article in question, that his skin started to tingle.

***

It was a good thing, thought Simon as he crossed the first canal, that he'd come downstairs with a coat that also had a hood – on waking, he'd seen how wet the day was – otherwise he'd be getting soaked. Whereas now he was more than adequately protected against anything the skies might chuck at him.

Less so against the facts of his position, however, and it didn't help either that he and Margaret – this morning he was finding it difficult to think of her as just Mum; Auntie M was history; plain Margaret would have to do – should have exchanged such angry words. He came to another canal and began to walk beside it, water to his left, a row of tall and gracious town houses to his right. It had all seemed so simple outside Notre Dame. So simple, so correct; pre-ordained almost. Because he wanted Margaret to be his mum. No question about that. But then, as the day progressed, although everything stayed okay on the surface, internally was another matter. He'd started to re-examine certain aspects of his life story, then had come the sleepless night, then a *contretemps* with Margaret and now nothing was quite as simple anymore. Or as secure. If one thread in a pattern is pulled, you run the risk of an entire unravelling.

The truth was: he resented being denied a father. That was the nub of it. He imagined that things, a great many things, might have turned out quite, quite otherwise had there been a constant and stable male figure in his life.

(Not that his father sounded stable. All the same. Knowing he was father to Simon might have altered that. To a degree. You could always hope.)

With this in mind, Simon found himself revisiting certain pivotal moments. That school skiing trip for instance, which Margaret, in her role as Auntie M, had paid for, and being in the snow with Richard. All that he'd in fact felt when it came to bloody Richard! If he'd known a proper father, instead of a poor copy in Henry, would he have been quite so vulnerable to the likes of a Richard? He doubted it.

Or was he fooling himself here? Was the lack of a proper father incidental? He'd never know for sure, of course he wouldn't, there were too many imponderables, too many blind alleys, and yet, and yet – he still couldn't help thinking that if he'd been granted access to his real dad, all might have been different. *He* might have been different.

Which then led him to consider Alison and his relationship with her and why, after she'd told him about falling in love with one of her house-mates, a legal student called Helen, he'd not immediately revealed his own sexuality in return. And again – if things had been different, if he'd been different, surely he would have? Would have had the confidence to speak up at once. Surely? But being kept in the dark by Margaret, who'd all along been the custodian of his true identity and who now appeared reluctant to put him in touch with his dad, even supposing she could, because actually this Gustavo figure might prove difficult to trace, but anyway – how the hell did any of this do anything to help him when it came to getting a grip on who he truly was?

Or was he, in thinking along such muddled lines, merely trying to side-step ultimate responsibility for his own actions? Blame other factors instead of just himself?

Take Alison again: might the real reason for not daring to tell her about his matching sexuality be because then he'd have had to confess the full extent of the feelings he'd harboured for Richard over the years? The boyfriend she'd broken up with by text. The guy they both agreed was unworthy of attention. Was beneath contempt in fact.

He crossed another bridge and, after a while, came to yet another canal, similar to the last. But then this whole city had a uniformity about it; a pleasing coherence. Unlike the tangle called Simon!

So now he began thinking: maybe the fact that he'd not told Alison about himself had less to do with Richard *per se* than with wanting to hold off until he could reply in kind by saying that he too had someone in his life that he wasn't ashamed to talk about. Who made sense of things for him. Someone like Helen, although, in his case, male of course.

But when was *that* likely to happen? Given the tenuous hold he had on his own identity.

Oh, yes! He was a tangle all right. An awful, awful tangle.

And what the hell was he to do about any of it? How to unmuddle things? With Margaret. With himself.

What he required was a helping hand. Someone like that person he was hoping to tell Alison about.

In short, and on so many levels: what he needed in his life was a man!

This last thought carried him into a wide intersection just off the canal he'd been following and, as he began traversing it, so his skin started to tingle. He looked about him. Straight ahead was an ornately capped tower, built half of brick, half of stone, attached to a substantial building. All around were a number of even more substantial apartment or office blocks. There were tramlines on the road and corresponding cables overhead. And he had the sense – instantly the sense; inescapably the sense – that this was where his recurring dream was set.

Of course, in his dream the buildings were only the vaguest of shapes. Nothing like as detailed as this. But still – why else would his skin be tingling so?

Then he saw it. On the far side of the intersection. A figure in a dark blue raincoat. Hurrying towards him when, in his dream, it was always he who was hurrying towards the figure. Without ever managing to reach what he was after.

***

'My,' said Margaret, 'but you *are* a creature of habit!'

''Fraid so!'

'Don't you ever vary your diet?'

'Not if I can possibly avoid it. Not in the mornings anyway. As I see things...'

On leaving Cody, Geoffrey had helped himself to his usual orange juice, a piece of fruit, some muesli and a pot of vanilla yoghurt before then carrying his tray to the table in the corner where, as he'd already established on entering the room, Margaret was taking a final sip or two of her coffee. He'd sat down and arranged his breakfast to his liking in front of him and this was when Margaret had commented upon it. And because it was a safe subject among some very unsafe ones potentially – the brief but acute awkwardness Isobel had caused the evening before came to mind; Isobel with her big mouth and airy assumption that he and Margaret must be an item – he'd happily gone along with it and they'd ended up discussing at some length what might or might not constitute the ideal breakfast. It was only when Geoffrey began spooning some sugar into his coffee, which he'd been served by the same Romanian waitress as before – they'd exchanged a knowing smile; the word *zahăr* had been uttered – that he'd plucked up the courage to ask Margaret about Simon going AWOL, as Cody had so succinctly put it.

'I hope you don't mind me asking,' he said, 'but is everything okay? Has something happened to upset Simon that he should go off without waiting for the rest of us?'

Margaret seemed relieved to have been asked and at once told him all about their argument – 'although I'm not sure argument is quite the right word' – over the not insignificant matter of Gustavo. The boy's missing father.

'And my dilemma, my problem,' she concluded, 'is that even if I have to, even if I want to, which I'm not sure I do, but in any event, I can't guarantee being able to find him.'

While talking, she'd begun to look more and more troubled, which had the effect on Geoffrey of making him wish that Isobel had been right and they were indeed an item and he could just take her into his arms and assure her that everything was going to be all right. It would have been the most effective course of action.

As it was, however, all he had at his disposal were bloody words.

'We should have collared the rascal in Rome,' were the ones he settled upon.

She winced. 'Except was that for real? Or just another trick of Cody's?'

'What, you think that if you had actually spoken to him...?'

'Who knows, yes, he might have dematerialised.' A bitter smile came to her lips. 'Mind you, that would have been true to form where Gustavo's concerned. To vanish. Pouf! Into thin air. Just like that. And besides, it might not have been him at all. I can't be certain. So much time has elapsed. People do change.'

'Of course they do,' said Geoffrey. 'And I'm thinking also, interestingly enough, that there really isn't all that much resemblance between the pair of them. Simon and Gustavo, I mean. Is there now? You wouldn't know, just from looking at them, that they were father and son. Or not that I could see anyway, from our Roman encounter.'

'No, you're right, there isn't. He has some of Gustavo's looks, but not too many. Thank goodness! A hint of his smile maybe. But then my colouring, which, if I'm honest, I've always been rather grateful for. Otherwise it wouldn't have been nearly so feasible to pretend as we did. He would have stood out by a country mile. Being swarthy in Suffolk – dead bloody giveaway!'

Though as she made this wry observation, the expression on her face so totally contradicted the guilty satisfaction she was admitting to – she looked more troubled and distressed than ever – that before he knew it, Geoffrey had reached across the table and was squeezing both her hands in his.

'Going back to your dilemma,' he said, 'you can absolutely do it if you need to, you know. Easy peasy. Well, maybe easy's an exaggeration, but the internet's a wonderful tool for finding people.'

She was looking in some surprise at their conjoined hands.

'Really,' he went on. 'Believe me. It really is.'

'But only,' she said finally, 'only if you're familiar with it. Which sadly I'm not.'

'I could always help you.'

'You could?'

'In point of fact, we could even start while Cody's out hunting Simon. If you liked. Why put off until tomorrow what can be done today?'

As he spoke, she withdrew, but very slowly, her hands from his and was now staring at him most strangely. He knew therefore that the time had come, he could put it off no longer, to get Isobel's remark out into the open, where it could be fully accounted and apologised for. Much as it went against the grain to be saying sorry for something he secretly wished were true.

Taking a deep breath, he began by explaining that Isobel had always been one to speak out of turn. She'd a big mouth, had Isobel. Liked to use it too and Margaret was please to ignore all that had been implied in that Parisian bar. Think of it as another of Cody's less amenable, less useful tricks.

'Cody and his box of bloody tricks!' said Margaret. 'Surprises in every compartment. Nothing ever quite as you'd expect. Much to marvel at. Almost too much, in some cases.'

'Like,' said Geoffrey, 'and I was about to challenge him, as a matter of fact, in the lobby just now, then he rushed off to find Simon. But anyway, my novel, my short stories – I looked in my satchel this morning to check they were still there. Have a wee gloat, I suppose. And guess what? They've vanished. Dematerialised utterly, as you thought might happen with Gustavo. They only existed for a day.'

'Oh,' said Margaret. 'No! I am sorry, Geoffrey.'

'Actually,' he said, 'once I'd got over the shock, it actually made sense. For me they were a pointer, that's all. Some sort of signpost. They'd served their purpose. Yours too.'

'And we poor mortals,' added Margaret thoughtfully, 'we're not meant to know, I don't think, how it all works. We're at the receiving end. It's a test really of faith.'

Geoffrey chuckled. 'You and your Catholic way of seeing things!'

Smiling faintly in response, she replied with: 'But we were talking about your indiscreet ex-wife. Tell me more, please. If you can. *And* about her husband, who used to be your lodger, didn't you say once? Am I remembering right?'

'You most certainly are. But why would you want…?'

'She's clearly a force to be reckoned with and I'm interested in how you managed it.'

'Ah, but did I though? That's the million dollar question.'

'Let me be the judge of that.'

And so, precisely as if this were his day in court (or an especially extensive journal entry), Geoffrey started for the second time in as many days on the story of himself and Isobel. Going into even more detail this time than he had with Cody after their visit to the wax museum. He spoke of how they'd met at a friend's party and how he'd not realised that she'd actually come with a boyfriend and so had boldly kissed her on the stairs. Which she'd not minded, he was quick to point out. Isobel approved of boldness.

He described the happiness of those early days, their many hopes and dreams, the fun and the laughter. The lightness. Also a basement flat in Stoke Newington, with Howard as their lodger and Isobel starting on her career as an economist. In which capacity, she'd become so successful that soon they'd been able to swap the flat for a whole house without the encumbrance of a lodger. Though Howard did remain in their lives, having attached himself to them in a limpet-like way that Geoffrey would only fully uncover many years later. Meanwhile, in the big, empty and new house, which they'd bought with children in mind, they quickly discovered that they couldn't produce any of those and so Isobel worked ever harder at her career, rising ever higher, while Geoffrey just went on teaching. Teaching and, at the same time, watching his own dreams of becoming a successful writer wither slowly away. Not an easy existence, for all that they were materially secure.

Here Geoffrey paused. Then he said: 'Once upon a time I used to think of Isobel as my nemesis. Like you with Rome. And in those days I would have told you in exhaustive detail how she challenged and mocked and made me miserable. Before running off with a bastard called Howard whom, as I say, she'd even slept with at the start of our marriage. But thanks to Paris, to Cody and to Paris, I've come to appreciate that she had her reasons, good reasons too, for behaving as she did. She'd married a man she thought was going somewhere. A man who would give her children. And while the last bit can't be helped, the rest most certainly can. All in all, I was a terrible coward, I see that now, and quite rightly, she held me to account. And while we're on the subject, Howard's not such a bastard either. He's actually all right, in the final analysis, is Howard. I'm the real disappointment.'

'Aren't you being a little too harsh on yourself?'

'I don't think so.'

'Well I do!' said Margaret stoutly. 'And if *you're* a coward, then what the hell does that make me? Look at the mess *I've* made of things! Poor Simon, no wonder he's so upset.' Her fingers began fiddling with the teaspoon that lay on the saucer of her empty coffee cup. 'You were quite right just now to tease me.'

'Tease you?'

'About my faith. I need to take a long hard look at how and why I've arrived at certain things. It's my beliefs, see, in part anyway, that are responsible for holding Simon back. For making him hide his true self.' Here she faltered. 'Oh dear,' she continued after a moment's pause, 'I'm not so sure I should be saying any of this.'

'Then don't.'

'But I need to share it with someone.'

'Then do.'

She set aside her teaspoon. 'And you were good enough to listen in Rome. You are indeed a fine listener. Nothing lacking in the ear department where you're concerned!'

'Thank you!' It's one thing, he was thinking, to say something of yourself; quite another to have it so sweetly confirmed.

Meanwhile, she was looking at him beseechingly. 'But can I trust you not to mention anything afterwards to anyone? Especially Simon.'

'Of course.'

'Because it's really not my place to be sharing his confidences.'

'You have my word. Go on, please.'

'Well, ever since he spoke to me on the boat about...'

To Geoffrey, it felt as if some sort of internal loosening was underway in Margaret and so, partly because he wanted to show encouragement, but also for more personal reasons, he extended a hand and quietly took hold again of the fingers that had just released the teaspoon. Simultaneously, in his role as good listener, he was paying keen attention as she began telling him how, on the boat they'd taken across that lake in Switzerland, Simon had announced that he was gay. Which had come as a complete surprise, she said, although in thinking about it afterwards, perhaps not so much. She just wished she knew him better than she obviously did. But what could one expect? Having missed so much of his childhood. Still, thanks in no small part to Geoffrey, at least she had then managed to tell Simon who his real mother was. End of story, you might have thought, and for a while so it had seemed. But as with everything in life, one thing inevitably leads to another and now she was having to look at whole other swathes of herself and she didn't always like what she saw. Not one bit.

She asked Geoffrey whether he recalled Simon's description of the snow from his school skiing trip? As a blank canvas. A phrase which, for many reasons, had always resonated with her. Never more so than now, representing as it did the possibility of new perspectives, new patterns. A fresh start.

'It's been such a strange week,' she said. 'So much has shifted. And if we're not careful, the opportunities we've been given, they'll all be snatched away again. Isobel's right. We must be bold. Grasp the future with both hands.' All of which she uttered without ever specifying just what opportunities she meant, or bold in what way.

Not that Geoffrey needed specifics. The grasping he got and he reached out in consequence with his other hand and so it was that the Romanian waitress, who happened at that moment to be passing with a jug of coffee for another table, noticed how Margaret lost no time in clutching it. The sight triggered a singular train of thought in the waitress, who'd seen a number of noteworthy things in her first week of work at this new hotel in what was also a new city for her, but none as touching as this. It reminded her of a painting she'd come across in the Rijksmuseum, where – since she hoped one day to be able to study art, after she'd put enough aside – she'd gone on her afternoon off. She didn't remember who the painting was by, but it was of a richly robed man and a slightly younger woman standing side by side, wholly absorbed in each other, and it was one of the tenderest she'd ever seen. Love personified, for the watcher, in every glowing detail. And now here was a similar degree of tenderness, albeit on a smaller scale, between this much older woman and the kind man who liked to ask for sugar in Romanian and who'd taken the trouble to seek her out and thank her after she'd almost spilled the contents of her tray over them on her very first day in the job.

***

As he strode through Amsterdam's wet streets, crossing first one bridge and then another, going from canal to canal, always on the lookout, the tingling that had started up when Cody had donned the blue raincoat was all the time intensifying and he was being made to feel ever more aware of his predicament. Margaret had sent him out into the rain to find Simon because she needed her son to know how deeply he was loved. End of story. But if Cody were to now heed the tingling and follow some promptings of his own, how did that square with what Margaret wanted? Or with what Simon himself might require? Quite apart from how he, Cody, in his role as tour leader, was supposed to be acting!

With every bridge crossed, every canal reached, he became increasingly uncomfortable, increasingly impatient, increasingly suspicious. Uncomfortable as to his predicament; impatient as to its solution; suspicious that there was more in play here than met the eye. The blue raincoat, for instance. Whose was it? Why had Simon noticed it on the first day of their trip? And why had it still been there a whole week later? Never mind the tingling.

But what was he to do, actually do, about any of this? Could any of it have been avoided? If, say, he'd kept his head down to a greater extent and simply got on with the job in hand, not letting its many demands upset him as they had, would that have made a difference? Possibly. He'd have been less vulnerable, that's for certain. But could he have switched off entirely? He didn't think so. At which point, he came to an open intersection beside the canal he'd been following and there a certain person was, slap bang in the centre of it. Solitary, motionless, surprised. Looking in Cody's direction in manifest amazement. Or was it alarm Cody could see on Simon's face? At that distance, it was hard to be sure.

He broke into a trot.

'There you are!' he began, on reaching Simon's side, where he could now tell that all of the emotions he'd just witnessed, and then some, were in evidence. 'Are you okay?'

'Awesome!' was Simon's response. His voice sounded oddly hushed.

'Sorry?'

'This is what my dream has always been moving me towards.'

And that was when it happened. Cody found himself in the tightest of embraces, from which he felt there was no chance of escape. Not that he wanted to escape; the sensation was too warm for that, too welcome. For the longest of delicious and startled moments, he felt less alone than he ever had before.

He didn't dare move. Nor did he speak. It was Simon who broke the silence.

'Because you're my dream figure, right,' he explained, dropping the words into Cody's ear as a whisper. 'I just couldn't see clearly before.'

And now Cody did pull back at last to murmur humorously: 'I bet that's what you've been wanting to say to all the boys!'

After the amazement and the fright, they were both beginning to smile a little.

'No, really!' said Simon, keeping a close grip on Cody's arm. 'Remember when we were in that park in Rome? I told you about this dream I have, where I'm in some sort of a square or an open space and it's all rather threatening...'

'And I said that dreams were beyond my remit.'

'Exactly! But anyway, when I arrived here just now, this place, I knew immediately *this* was the place, it just had to be. Don't ask me how, because in my dream the details are all quite hazy and I sense rather than see the buildings. Except that recently there's been some lapping of water and here we are by a canal. Also, in the rain. Anyway, the point is, I just knew this is where my dream always brings me and the moment I realised this, that was when I saw you.' He tightened his grip on Cody. 'And what I didn't tell you when we spoke about it in Rome was that the figure in my dream, the one who's actually my only hope of ever getting out of the square safely, the one I never manage to reach, is in a blue raincoat. Like the one you're wearing now. And in fact, I saw another just like it at the start of our trip, on a stand by the main door to the hotel. Although in my dream, it's always me who's doing the running. Not like now, when you came in my direction. Can you believe this?'

There was a long, considered pause. Then, smile widening, Cody nodded. 'Every word!'

'Because I couldn't make it up.'

'No,' agreed Cody. 'Of course you couldn't. To make up something like this, you need another sort of person altogether.' Like the one I happen to work for, he was thinking. Who'd recently instructed him not to feel even slightly obliged.

'And do you mind?' Simon sounded suddenly anxious. 'Being – I don't know how else to put it – being in my dream? Because if all of this is just in my own head, then naturally...'

Simon had by this stage relaxed his grip on Cody's arm and so now it was Cody's turn to grasp Simon's.

'God, no!' he cried, still smiling. 'My head too. Truly! You asked me once, if you remember, why we'd started in Amsterdam. And to be honest, I wasn't sure. But now I get it. You're the reason. This is where your dream takes place – and if I'm to be the one who steps into it, then we have to be somewhere where that can happen. Where the blue raincoat is. Nothing else makes any sort of sense.'

And just as Simon had clasped Cody to him earlier, Cody now pulled Simon into a tight embrace and their new reality assumed its human form.

'Although in point of fact,' Simon said softly, again into Cody's ear, 'this isn't the first time we've been alone together in a square. There was also the Piazza Navona. After Geoffrey had gone looking for Margaret. That was awesome too.'

'Margaret!' echoed a stricken Cody, who'd almost forgotten. 'She's desperate for you to know something.' He pulled Simon even closer. 'It breaks her heart, she says, to think that anything might ever come between the two of you. You're her son. She's your mother. End of story.' Adding, with a throaty chuckle: 'Now give us another of those smiles! Has anyone ever told you what a really great smile it is? You should trot it out more often.'

***

Back at the hotel, Margaret and Geoffrey had settled themselves on the couch in the lobby, where they'd sat once before when she'd told him all about the Barrie play her godfather had so liked. *Dear Brutus*. And it was about this old play that she was speaking again now.

'As I think I told you,' she said, 'what they discovered, Barrie's characters, was that they hadn't really changed. They all still carried their baggage with them. But after this little trip of ours, like I said earlier, I do feel that things have shifted. Materially shifted. Nothing's ever going to be the same again.'

'And is that frightening, as a thought? Or good?'

'Well, there's lots that still needs sorting out, that's for sure. But overall? Overall: good, I think. We've not been given too hard a ride. Lucky old us.'

Neither of them had noticed that standing by the desk was an elderly gentleman in a crumpled linen suit, the whiteness of which had long since yellowed with age. Nor did they register it as his eyes, which were a piercing green, swept over them. Though Margaret did shiver suddenly, as if caught in a draught.

'Yes,' grinned Geoffrey. 'I'm thinking that when I get back, I'm going to hand in my notice.'

'You are?'

'Foolish of me, maybe, at this stage of life, but what the hell! And yourself? If Simon's going to university, then as I've already suggested, I really do think you should consider returning to your own studies. I'll never forget standing with you in front of those paintings and how you reacted to them. The Rembrandt and – the Raphael, was it?'

Margaret nodded. '*La Fornarina*. Whom you called, I think, one very sexy lady.'

'Well, she was!'

'Gustavo felt the same.' Inwardly, she was smiling. Two Gs. Gustavo. Geoffrey. Such linguistic neatness!

The revolving door swung into action and through it came Simon and Cody while, at the same time, the elderly gentleman by the desk took a step forward. Although he still remained unobserved by the others for the moment. Cody was too busy hanging the blue raincoat back where he'd found it. Margaret was fussing over Simon. And Geoffrey, having also risen to his feet, was focused totally on Simon and Cody, who'd finally joined them by the couch. Was it his imagination, or did the pair of them appear, albeit subtly, to be behaving differently towards each other?

Then Cody clapped his hands. 'So how about,' he asked, 'another group photo? Before we begin deciding what we'd like to do with the rest of the day?'

They heard a cough behind them and a reedy voice said: 'Excuse me, but I couldn't help overhearing. May I be of assistance?'

As one, they turned and found that an elderly gentleman in a crumpled linen suit had come up to where they were clustered.

The gentleman addressed himself to Cody. 'Then you can be in it too, for once. So pass me your phone, why don't you, and if you'll all just stand against the couch... Yes, that's right... Closer!... Say cheese!... Good... And another for luck.'

'Thank you,' said Geoffrey as, with a courteous flourish, the gentleman handed Cody back his phone.

'My pleasure. Happy to be of some service.'

At which precise juncture, the doors to the lift slid open and out poured a fresh group of chattering Chinese who, in their cacophonous advance across the lobby, swept the old man away.

'And now, Simon, darling,' Margaret was saying. 'Don't you think you should go upstairs and change out of those wet trousers? You don't want to go home with a cold. Do you now? You too, Cody, if I may be so bold.'

Cody wasn't listening, however. He was still scouring the lobby for some sign of their departed photographer. But already Cedric had vanished. Something else had gone too. The coat-stand by the door was now empty. They'd been left to their own devices.

Acknowledgments

I owe thanks to many friends and to my family for their ongoing support, Peter especially. Also to Laura Morris and some crucial early readers. You know who you are.

About the Author

Tony Peake was born and educated in South Africa. He moved to London in the early seventies. He has worked in the theatre as a production manager, briefly as a model, as a teacher and then for many years as a literary agent. He currently spends most of his time, when not travelling, in North East Essex, where he lives with his civil partner.

He is the author of *Derek Jarman: The Authorised Biography* (Little, Brown, 1999; Abacus, 2001; Allison & Busby, 2025) and three novels: *A Summer Tide* (Abacus, 1993), *Son to the Father* (Little, Brown, 1995; Abacus, 1996) and *North Facing* (Myriad Editions, 2017). As a prize-winning short story writer and occasional essayist, his work has been widely anthologised and he has also edited a collection of short stories on the theme of *Seduction* (Serpent's Tail, 1994). Further details on: www. tonypeake.com

Other Novels by Tony Peake

North Facing

For one long, intense week in October 1962, the Cuban Missile Crisis brought with it an East-West stand-off and the possibility of nuclear holocaust. On the other side of the globe, in Pretoria, a group of schoolboys scan the horizon for signs that the world is about to end. Many years later, one of their number, Paul Harvey, now in his sixties and living abroad, is drawn back to South Africa to confront the unexpected and chilling consequences of this seminal boyhood moment – and the part he unwittingly played in the drama that unfolded. (Myriad Editions 9780995590021)

"This beautiful, moving novel is vast in how much it recounts and how deeply it makes us feel."
— **Edmund White**

"A gracefully achieved work of art made more powerful by its quiet anger and understatement."
— **Shena Mackay**

"Tony Peake is in the top rank of South African writers right now."
— **David Willers**, *LitNet*

Son to the Father

When ten-year-old Jed unexpectedly lands a part in a film – to be shot in northern Spain by celebrated opera director Carlos Tarifa – his mother's close friend, Peter, gives up his teaching job to join Jacqui and Jed on set. In charting Peter's complex journey towards a sense of his own identity within this glittering and multi-faceted milieu, the novel explores themes of sex and spirituality, fatherhood, commitment and reconciliation. (Abacus 9780349108070)

"A brilliant and rapturous book."
— **Hugh Barnes**, *Glasgow Herald*

"[Tony Peake] writes with dry ease on the difficulty of being alive."
— **David Hughes**, *Mail on Sunday*

A Summer Tide
On an isolated island off the east coast of England, linked to the mainland only by a slim causeway, Lucy Hamilton's identity is disappearing as her beauty slowly wanes. Then into the lives of herself and her artist husband, Charles, there comes a stranger: a beautiful, sensual young man, whose own personality is an enigmatic secret. Suddenly Lucy's days are lit with anticipation – but darkened by the complex emotions that the young man's presence arouses, and the relationships it causes her to reassess. (Abacus 9780349105536)

"A controlled and subtly crafted novel that deals with a deep truth of human experience: flawed love that is yet worth struggling to preserve."
— **Barry Unsworth**

"All the best aspects of the English literary tradition are brought together here and woven into a bright whole."
— **Alma Hromic**, *Cape Argus*

**ROUNDFIRE
BOOKS**

FICTION

Put simply, we publish great stories. Whether it's literary or popular, a gentle tale or a pulsating thriller, the connecting theme in all Roundfire fiction titles is that once you pick them up you won't want to put them down.

If you have enjoyed this book, why not tell other readers by posting a review on your preferred book site.

The Cause
Roderick Vincent
The second American Revolution will be a
fire lit from an internal spark.
Paperback: 978-1-78279-763-0 ebook: 978-1-78279-762-3

Don't Drink and Fly
The Story of Bernice O'Hanlon: Part One
Cathie Devitt
Bernice is a witch living in Glasgow. She loses her way
in her life and wanders off the beaten track looking for the
garden of enlightenment.
Paperback: 978-1-78279-016-7 ebook: 978-1-78279-015-0

Gag
Melissa Unger
One rainy afternoon in a Brooklyn diner, Peter Howland
punctures an egg with his fork. Repulsed, Peter pushes
the plate away and never eats again.
Paperback: 978-1-78279-564-3 ebook: 978-1-78279-563-6

The Master Yeshua
The Undiscovered Gospel of Joseph
Joyce Luck
Jesus is not who you think he is. The year is 75 CE. Joseph
ben Jude is frail and ailing, but he has a prophecy to fulfil ...
Paperback: 978-1-78279-974-0 ebook: 978-1-78279-975-7

On the Far Side, There's a Boy
Paula Coston
Martine Haslett, a thirty-something 1980s woman, plays hard
on the fringes of the London drag club scene until one night
which prompts her to sign up to a charity. She writes to a
young Sri Lankan boy, with consequences far and long.
Paperback: 978-1-78279-574-2 ebook: 978-1-78279-573-5

Tuareg
Alberto Vazquez-Figueroa
With over 5 million copies sold worldwide, *Tuareg* is a classic
adventure story from best-selling author Alberto Vazquez-
Figueroa, about honour, revenge and a clash of cultures.
Paperback: 978-1-84694-192-4

Readers of ebooks can buy or view any of these bestsellers by
clicking on the live link in the title. Most titles are published
in paperback and as an ebook. Paperbacks are available in
traditional bookshops. Both print and ebook formats are
available online.

Find more titles and sign up to our readers' newsletter at
www.collectiveinkbooks.com/fiction